THE POWERFULL  L
BY ONE OF T
NEW
SARAH ZETTEL

THE QUIET INVASION

"Zettel's narrative strategy is to emphasize the [human/alien] parallels: each side has its idealists, its pragmatists, and its self-righteous manipulators of facts and factions. Readers . . . may find themselves caring deeply about both sides; Zettel even manages to wring pathos out of the demise of an alien city."
—**New York Times Book Review**

"Zettel gets better with every book . . . a fantastic tour of Venus, with plenty of fresh ideas, excitement, and all-out wonder on the itinerary."
—**Science Fiction Weekly**

"Presents an interesting alien race, a perplexing problem . . . and a masterful grasp of the subtleties and intricacies inherent in the situation."
—**Science Fiction Chronicle**

"A tight tale of mankind's first meeting with aliens. The aliens are three-dimensional characters with their own flaws and noble attributes, as are the humans."
—**Southern Pines Pilot (NC)**

"Zettel, as always, supplies her characters with complex motivations. . . . She is well on her way to becoming one of the major science fiction writers of the twenty-first century."
—**Tulsa World**

more . . .

ALSO BY SARAH ZETTEL
PLAYING GOD
Selected a Best Book for the Teen Age by
the New York Public Library

Also by Sarah Zettel

Reclamation
Fool's War
Playing God

Available from Warner Aspect

SARAH ZETTEL

THE QUIET INVASION

WARNER BOOKS

A Time Warner Company

WARNER BOOKS EDITION

Copyright ©2000 by Sarah Zettel
All rights reserved. No part of this book may be reproduced in any form or by any electronic or mechanical means, including information storage and retrieval systems, without permission in writing from the publisher, except by a reviewer who may quote brief passages in a review.

Aspect® name and logo are registered trademarks of Warner Books, Inc.

Cover design by Don Puckey
Cover illustration by Steve Youll

Warner Books, Inc.
1271 Avenue of the Americas
New York, NY 10020

Visit our Web site at
www.twbookmark.com

 A Time Warner Company

Printed in the United States of America

Originally published in hardcover by Warner Books
First Paperback Printing: March 2001

10 9 8 7 6 5 4 3 2 1

This book is dedicated, with deepest thanks,
to my spiritual big sister,
Dawn Marie Sampson Beresford.

Acknowledgments

The author would like to thank Timothy B. Smith for his expert technical advice, Laura Woody, who knew about the yeast, and Dr. David Grinspoon, whose *Venus Revealed* she consulted frequently during the writing of this book. She would also like to thank Betsy Mitchell and Jaime Levine, whose patient work made this a better book, and Karen Everson, who was there for the crisis.

THE QUIET INVASION

CHAPTER ONE

"This is Venera Control, Shuttle AX-2416. You're clear for landing. Welcome back."

Hello, Tori. How are you doing? thought Helen from her seat in the passenger compartment. She liked the fact that the shuttle pilots left the intercom open so she could listen to the familiar voices running through the landing protocols. Overhearing this final flight ritual made her feel that she was really home.

I just wish I was really home with better news.

She bit her lip and settled a little further back in her crashcouch. Helen was the only Venera-bound passenger this run. She'd flown from Earth in the long-distance ship *Queen Isabella*, which now waited in orbit while the shuttles from Venera ferried down supplies and equipment that had to be imported from Earth.

Helen stared straight ahead over the rows of empty couches. The ceiling and front wall of the shuttle's passenger cabin were one gigantic view screen. Venus's opaque, yellowish-gray clouds churned all around the shuttle. Wind stirred the mists constantly but never cleared them away.

She strained her eyes, struggling to see the solid shadow of

Venera Base through the shifting fog. Despite everything, Helen still felt as if she carried the bad news with her, that nothing could have changed aboard Venera until she got there and handed the news over.

I'm not there so it's not real yet. Helen smoothed down the indigo scarf she wore over her stark white hair. *Arrogance, arrogance, old woman. This last trip should have finally put you in your place.*

She really did feel old. It was strange. Even in the modern era of med trips and gene-level body modification, eighty-three was not young. She had never felt so old *inside,* though. She'd never felt calcified like this, as if something in her understanding had failed, leaving her standing on the edge of events she was unable to comprehend clearly, let alone affect.

The shuttle's descent steepened. At last, the cloud veil thinned enough that Helen really could make out the spherical shadow of Venera Base—her dream, her life's work, her home.

And now, my poor failure.

Even with self-pity and defeat swimming around inside her head, Helen's heart lifted at the sight of Venera. The base was a gigantic sphere buoyed by Venus's thick CO_2 atmosphere. Distance and cloud cover made the massive girders and cables that attached the tail and stabilizers to the main body of the station look as thin as threads.

Venera rode the perpetual easterly winds that circled the planet's equator. The shuttle matched Venera's speed easily, and the navigation chips in the shuttle and the runway handled the rest. The shuttle glided onto the great deck that encircled the very top of Venera's hull. It taxied straight across the runway and to the open hangar.

The shuttle jerked slightly as it rolled to a stop. A moment of silence enveloped Helen. This was no tourist shuttle. There were no attendants, human or automated, to tell her it was okay to get up now, or to make sure she claimed all her luggage, or to hope she'd enjoyed her flight and would come again soon.

Instead, the hissing, bumping noises of pressurization, corridor docking, and engine power-down surrounded her. Helen stayed where she was. As soon as she stepped out of the shuttle, it all became real. The transition would be over. Her illusions would no longer shield her. Helen found she did not want to abandon that shelter.

"Dr. Failia?"

Helen started and looked up into the broad, dark face of the shuttle's senior pilot. What was his name?

"Yes?" She pushed herself upright and began fumbling with the multiple buckles that strapped her to the couch. *Name, name, name . . .*

"I just wanted to say, I know you're going to get us through this. Everybody's with you."

Pearson! "Thank you, Mr. Pearson," said Helen. "We'll find a way."

"I know we will." He stepped aside to give her room to stand. Helen did not miss the hand that briefly darted out to help her to her feet and then darted back again, afraid of being offensive. She pretended to ignore the awkward gesture and retrieved her satchel from the bin under her couch.

"Thank you again, Mr. Pearson." Helen shook the pilot's hand and met his eyes with a friendly smile. *P.R. reflexes all in working order, thank you.*

Then, because there was nothing else to do, she walked down the flex-walled docking corridor.

Bennet Godwin and Michael Lum, the other two members of Venera's governing board, were, of course, waiting for her in the passenger clearing area. One look at their faces told her that the bad news had indeed flown far ahead of her.

Her hand tightened around her satchel strap as she walked up to her colleagues.

"I take it you've heard," she said flatly. "We lost Andalucent Technologies and IBM." *There, it's official. I said it.* The last shards of her comforting illusions fell away.

Ben Godwin was a square-built, florid man. Every emotion registered on his face as a change of color, from snow white to cherry red. Right now though, he just looked gray. He opened his mouth, but nothing came out.

Michael, standing beside him, glanced briefly at the floor and then up at Helen's eyes. He was a much younger, much leaner, much calmer man with clear gold skin. He wore his black hair long and pulled back into a ponytail. The gold ID badge on his white tunic proclaimed him the chief of Venera's security. "They took the University of Washington with them."

He spoke softly, but the words crashed hard against Helen. "What? When?"

"About an hour ago." Ben ran his hand over his bristly scalp. "We tried to get them to wait to talk to you, but they weren't—"

Anger hardened Helen's face. "Well, they'll have to talk to me anyway." She brushed past the two men. "We can't afford to lose their funding too."

Helen did not look back to see if they were following her. She just strode straight ahead into the broad, curving corridor that connected the docking area to the rest of Venera. She ignored the nearest elevator bundle and started down the stairs instead. She was not waiting around anymore. She'd been waiting on people for months on Earth. Waiting for them to tell her they had no more money, no more time to wait for results, no more interest in a planet that would never be amenable to human colonization or exploitation.

Helen kept her office on the farm levels near the center of

Venera's sphere. Full spectrum lights shone down on vast soil beds growing high-yield cereals and brightly colored vegetables. Ducks and geese waded freely through troughed rice paddies that also nurtured several species of fish. The chickens, however, were penned in separate yards around the perimeter. The chickens did not get along with the more peaceable fowls. Quartz windows ringed the entire level, showing the great gray clouds. Every now and then, a pure gold flash of sheet lightning lit the world.

The farms had been meant to give Venera some measure of independence. Acquiring good, fresh food was vital to the maintenance of a permanent colony, and from the beginning, Helen had meant Venera to be a permanent colony.

Old dreams died hard. Venera might have actually had real self-sufficiency, except for the restrictions the U.N. placed on manufacturing and shipping licenses.

Old fears died hard too.

Helen's office was an administrative cubicle on an island in the middle of one of the rice paddies. She knew people called it "the Throne Room" and didn't really care. She loved Venus, but she missed Earth's blues and greens. Setting up her workspace in the farms had been the perfect compromise.

Helen kept a spartan office. It was furnished with a work desk, three visitor's chairs, and an all-purpose view screen that currently showed a star field. Her one luxury, besides her view, was a couple of shelves of potted plants—basil, oregano, lavender, and so on. Their sweet, spicy scents were the air's only perfume.

Helen dropped herself into the chair behind the desk and tossed her satchel onto the floor. It was only then that she became aware that Michael and Ben had in fact followed her.

"Who'd you talk to?" Her touch woke the desk and lit its command board. She shuffled through the icons to bring up her list of contact codes.

"Patricia Iannone," said Ben, sitting in one of the visitor's chairs. "She sounded like she was just following orders."

"We'll see." Helen activated Pat's contact and checked the time delay. Four minutes today. Not great for purposes of persuasive conversation, but doable. Helen opened the com system and lifted her face to the view screen. "Hello, Pat. I've just gotten back to Venera, and they're telling me that U Washington is pulling our funding. What's the matter? You can't tell me the volcanology department has not been getting its money's worth out of us. If it's a matter of being more vocal about your sponsorship or about allowing your people some more directed research time, I know we can work out the details. You just have to let me know what you and your people need." She touched the Send key, and the com system took over, shooting the message down after the contact code, waiting for a connection, and a reply.

Helen swiveled her chair to face Ben and Michael. "All right, tell me what's been happening since we talked last."

So Ben told her about some of the new personnel assignments and promotions and how the volcano, Hathor Montes, was showing signs of entering an active cycle. Michael talked about a rash of petty thefts, an increase in demands on the data lines caused apparently by the volcanology group gearing up for Hathor's active cycle, and a couple of in-stream clip-out personas trying to get themselves inserted onto Venera's payroll.

"Now that would be all we'd need," muttered Helen. "Handing out extra money for a couple of computer ghosts."

As she spoke, the desk chimed. All of them turned their attention back to the view screen. Helen's stomach tightened. The star field cleared away to show a fashionably slim, young-looking woman with beige skin and a cloud of dark-blond hair, worn unbound under a pink scarf.

"Hello, Helen," she said soberly. "I was expecting this. Listen, there are no complaints about the publicity, the facilities access, about anything. The problems are application, opportunity, and resource distribution. The comptrollers have decided our people are going to have to be content with St. Helens and Pelée for a while. The industrial research spillover is contracting, and there is just not enough to go around right now." Her expression flickered from annoyed to apologetic. "There's no more after this. Anything you send is going to my machine. I'm sorry, but there is nothing I can do."

The stars faded back into view. For a moment, Helen met Ben's gaze, but she looked quickly away. She didn't want to see what he was thinking. *We could have done this,* he was thinking, *if you'd been willing to do it small. If you hadn't insisted from the beginning on a full-scale base where people could live and raise their children and make a lifetime commitment to the study of this world.*

She pressed her fingertips against her forehead. That was what he was thinking. That Venus was, at most, four weeks away from Earth. It wouldn't have mattered if people had to come and go. Venera could have been made small and simple and then expanded if things worked out. But, oh, no. Helen Failia had her vision, and Helen Failia had to push it through. Helen had to make sure there were children like Michael who could lose their homes if the funding ever collapsed.

"There is a way out of this," said Michael. "There has to be."

"What?" Helen's hand jerked away from her face. "Michael, I'm open to suggestions. I've just spent four months scavenging the whole of Mother Earth for additional funding. It's not there."

"Well." Michael rolled his eyes toward the ceiling and then brought them back down to meet Helen's gaze. "Have you tried a com burst out to Yan Su on the Colonial Affairs Committee? There might be some U.N. money we can dredge up."

Ben snorted. "Oh, come on, Michael. The U.N. pay to keep a colony running? Their business is keeping colonies scraping and begging." As a younger man, Helen knew, Ben had been strongly sympathetic with the Bradbury Separatist movement on Mars—the same movement that had blossomed into the Bradbury Rebellion and, for five short, violent years, Bradbury Free Territory. Because of that, he still took a very dim view of the United Nations and their off-Earth colonial policies.

She had to admit he was partly right. Since the Bradbury Rebellion, the C.A.C.'s sole function had been to make sure nothing like that ever happened again. Hence, the licensing restrictions. No colony could manufacture space shuttles or long-distance ships. No colony could manufacture communications satellites, although they were graciously allowed to repair the ones they had. There was a whole host of other hardware and spare parts that either never got licensed or were taxed to the Sun and back again.

Most of the time that didn't bother Helen. She dealt with the C.A.C. through her friend Yan Su, and so far Su had been willing to help whenever she could. Now, though, they were coming head-to-head with the old, frightened public policies.

"You think they want to deal with ten thousand refugees?" countered Michael calmly. "It's got to be cheaper to let us stay where we're at than to pay for processing ten thousand new resident-citizen files."

Helen nodded absently. She found, to her shame, she was not ready to admit that that avenue had been shut off almost a year ago. Maybe she could try again. *Now is not the time for pride,* she reminded herself firmly. *You've begged everybody else. Why not the government?*

"Yan Su helped put us up here," said Michael, more to Ben than to Helen. "Maybe she can help keep us up here." Ben's only response was to turn a little pinker and look sour.

As little as she liked to admit it, Michael was right. It was time for last resorts. Without their three major funding sources, they were not going to be able to meet their payroll. They could buy some time by laying off the nonpermanent residents and sending them back to Mother Earth, but then they wouldn't be able to complete their research projects and they'd lose yet more money.

Helen looked at the time delay again. Venus and Earth were moving out of conjunction. If she put this off, the time delay was only going to get worse, and she didn't want to have to conduct this conversation through the mail. "Why don't you—"

Movement outside the office cleared the door's view panel. Grace Meyer stood in front of the door with her arms folded and her impatience plain on her heavily lined face. Helen suppressed a groan. What she wanted to do was open the intercom and say, "We're having a meeting, Grace. Not now." But she held back. Grace had proven herself willing to make trouble lately, and Venera did not need more trouble.

"We'll finish in a minute, gentlemen," she said instead. "Door. Open. Hello, Grace," she said, not bothering to put on a smile, as Grace would know it was false. "What can I do for you?"

Dr. Grace Meyer was a short woman with a milk-and-roses complexion. Her lab coat was no longer crisp, and her tunic and trousers were as rumpled as if she'd slept in them. She wore a green kerchief tied over her short hair, which was the same strawberry blond as when she'd moved to Venera fifteen years ago. Grace was a long-lifer. She was actually twice Helen's age, even though she looked only half that old.

Grace nodded to Ben and Michael and then turned all her attention to Helen. "I heard about U Washington."

Helen sighed. "The only thing that travels faster than bad news is bad news about you personally." Ben and Michael did not smile. Ben looked grim. Michael looked like he was trying to calculate the probable outcome of this scenario so he could ready his responses.

"What about U Washington?" asked Helen.

Grace glanced at Ben and Michael. In that glance, Helen read that Grace would like to ask them to leave but couldn't quite work out how. *And I'll be damned if I'll help you,* Helen thought.

"Helen," Grace started again, "there are still sources of money out there. If we shift emphasis just a little—"

Here it comes. "To the possibility of life on Venus?"

Grace leaned across the desk. "You saw my new grant from Biotech 24. That's good money, Helen. The absorbers—"

"Are a complex set of benzene rings with some strange sulfuric hangers-on under heat and pressure."

Grace was a chemist who had come to Venera to help look for the ultraviolet absorber in the Venusian clouds. The clouds were mostly transparent to ultraviolet, but there were bands and patches that absorbed all but the very lowest end of the UV wavelengths. For years, no one had been able to work out what was happening. Grace and her team had isolated a large, complex carbon, oxygen, sulfur molecule that interacted with the sulfuric acid in the clouds and the UV from the Sun, so it was constantly breaking apart, re-forming and re-creating more of itself. Which was fine; it had won her awards and acclaim, and brought Venera a lot of good publicity.

The problem was, Grace was trying to get the compound, which she called "the absorber" for simplicity's sake, classified as life.

Helen got slowly to her feet. She was not tall, but she had a few centimeters on Grace and didn't mind using them. Especially now. She did not need this. "Your absorbers are not life. No funding university or independent research lab we've

had on board for the last ten years has said it could be quali-
fied as life, or even proto-life."

Grace held her ground. "But there's—"

"There's one little company that's got more of an existence
in-stream than out in reality. It's willing to gamble on your
idea this is some kind of alien autocatalytic RNA." Grace subsided just a little, but Helen wasn't ready to. The past months
had been too much on top of the past year, all the past years.
All the fighting, all the frustration, all the time wasted, *wasted*
on stupid, petty money-grubbing and useless personal projects. "I've read your papers, Grace. I've read them all, and
you know what? I wish I'd tried harder to get you to leave it
alone. You've directly contributed to the image of this base as
a useless piece of dreamware. You have cost us, Grace. You
personally have cost all of us!"

The intercom chimed again. "What is it?" demanded Helen
icily. She needed to take the call. She needed to stop yelling
at Grace. She was falling out of control, and she could not afford that. Grace could still make trouble—publicize internal
dissension, that kind of thing. There was plenty she could do.
Plenty she would do. Helen needed to stop.

"Ummm . . . Dr. Failia?" The screen flickered to life to
show a slender young man with clear, sandy-brown skin and
thick black hair. Behind him, a floor-to-ceiling view screen
displayed the ragged gray cliff, possibly the edge of one of the
continent-sized plateaus that broke the Venusian crust.

"Yes, Derek?" Helen tried to smooth the impatience out of
her voice. Derek Cusmanos headed the survey department.
Actually, Derek and his fleet of drones *were* the survey department. He always did his job well. He had done nothing to
deserve her anger.

"I . . . I'm getting some pictures in from one of the drones
near Beta Regio that you need to see, Dr. Failia."

Helen's fingers twitched as she tried not to clench her

hands into fists. "This is not a good time, Derek. Shoot me up a file and I'll go over it—"

"No, Dr. Failia." Strain tightened Derek's voice. "You really need to see this right now."

Curiosity and concern surfaced together in Helen's mind. She glanced back at Ben and Michael, who both returned blank stares. A glance at Grace produced a shrug and a pair of spread hands.

"All right, Derek," said Helen. "Show me."

Without another word, Derek pushed his chair back so they had a clear view of his wall screen. Helen heard him give soft orders to his desk to display the current uplink.

The screen's view changed. The gigantic plateau wall receded into the distance. In its place stood a smaller, rounded canyon wall, the kind that typically bordered the ancient lava channels. On the canyon's cracked floor, Helen saw something sticking up out of the ground. Derek gave another order. The view zoomed in.

The new, tighter view showed a perfectly circular shaft protruding from the Venusian ground.

"Oh my God," whispered Michael. Helen just got out of her chair and walked slowly forward until her nose almost touched the intercom screen.

It was not anything that should have been there, but there it was. It was circular. It had a cap on it. Its gray sides glinted dully in Venus's ashen light, and it sank straight into the bedrock.

"This is live," said Derek from his post off-screen. "I'm getting this in right now from SD-25."

"You've done a diagnostic?" cut in Ben. He supervised Derek's "department." "The drone is functioning on spec?"

"On spec and in the green," said Derek. "I . . . I didn't believe what I was seeing, so I sent SD-24 down after it. This is what I'm getting from SD-24." He gave another order and the view shifted again. Now they looked down from above, as if the camera drone perched on the canyon wall, which it probably did.

The capped shaft sat there, smooth and circular and utterly impossible. Even Venus, which had produced stone formations seen nowhere else in the solar system, had not created those smooth lines, that flattened lid.

"Well," said Ben. "I don't remember putting that there."

"Derek," said Helen quietly, "I want you to keep both drones on-site. I want that thing recorded from every possible angle. I want it measured and I want its dimensions and position to the millimeter. We'll get a scarab down there to look at it."

"Yes, Dr. Failia." Derek sounded relieved that someone else was making the decisions.

"Well done, young man," she added.

"Thank you, Dr. Failia."

The intercom cut out and Helen turned slowly around. "Do I have to say it?" she asked dryly.

"You mean that if that's what it looks like—" began Ben.

"We have evidence of life on Venus?" Grace folded her arms. Her green eyes gleamed brightly. "Oh, please, Helen. I'd love to hear you say it, just once."

A muscle in Helen's temple spasmed. "Now is not the time to be petty, Grace."

Grace smiled. "Oh no, not petty, Helen. But you'll have to allow me a little smugness. I've been shouting in the wilderness for years now. If this bears out—"

"*If* this bears out." Ben emphasized the first word heavily. "Venus has thrown up some landscapes that make the old face on Mars look passé." He pushed himself to his feet. "Kevin is on shift. I'll have him outfit us a scarab ay-sap." Kevin Cusmanos was Derek's older brother. He was also chief engineer and pilot for the surface-to-air explorer units known as scarabs, which transported people to and from the Venusian surface. "I assume you're coming down to see what's what?" Ben looked pointedly at Helen.

"Of course," she answered. "And Michael's coming with us." She looked to him for approval and he nodded. His face held a kind of stunned wonder as the implications filtered through him. Helen knew exactly how he felt. If this was played out, it meant so many things. It meant human beings were not alone in the universe. It meant there was not only intelligent life out there somewhere but it had also left its traces on Venus.

It meant money for Venera.

Grace opened her mouth, but Helen held up her hand. "Not this run, Grace. Next one, if it turns out to be more than rocks and heat distortion." *Keep up the patter, Helen. You do not know what's really down there. You only know what it looks like.*

Somewhat to Helen's surprise, Grace just nodded and stepped aside for Ben as he hurried out the door. Helen did not, however, miss the purely triumphant smile that spread across her face.

Can't blame her, I suppose. "If that's what it looks like," she repeated out loud.

"If that's what it looks like, all our old problems are over with, and we'll have a set of brand-new ones," said Michael. "But ohmygod . . ."

Helen touched his arm. "I quite agree. Go grab your gear, Michael, and tell Jolynn and the boys you won't be home for supper."

"Yes, ma'am." He snapped a mock salute and hurried out the door.

Grace and Helen faced each other for a long moment. "Well," said Grace brightly, "I think I'll go reorganize my files. I think there's going to be some new work coming in." She left, and the door slid shut behind her.

Finally alone, Helen reached up and untied her scarf. Her long white hair fell down around her shoulders. She combed her fingers through it, feeling how each strand separated and fell, brushing her cheeks and shoulders. It felt coarser than she remembered it feeling when she was a young woman. Coarser and yet more fragile, like its owner.

Let this work out, she prayed silently. *I don't care if I have to spend the next fifty years apologizing to Grace Meyer. This could save us all. Please, let it work out right.*

Less than five hours later, Helen, too on edge to remember she ought to be tired and hungry, unstrapped herself from a second crash-couch. This one was in the little dormitory aboard Scarab Fourteen. The scarab itself crawled across the Venusian surface, following the signal output of Derek Cusmanos's two drones.

Because it was Kevin Cusmanos's policy to always have two of Venera's twenty scarabs ready to go in case of emergency, heading to the surface had been a matter of grabbing overnight bags and calling on Adrian Makepeace, the duty pilot for the afternoon shift. Kevin said he'd take the board down himself, but he wanted Adrian's experience in the copilot's seat.

Scarab Fourteen was a clone of all the other scarabs owned and operated by Venera Base—a wedge-shaped, mobile laboratory that could both fly and roll. They were designed to take a team of up to seven researchers plus two crew members to almost any spot on the Venusian surface that wasn't covered in lava. Built wide and low to the ground, they were practical but not comfortable. Adrian, Helen noticed, seemed to be developing a permanent stoop and a tendency to walk sideways from all the time he spent in them.

Designing for the heat and pressure of the Venusian surface had proved incredibly difficult. That was one of the reasons Venera floated through the clouds. The surface was an oven. Up in the clouds, the temperature was close to the freezing point of water. Down here, they had to carry layers of insulation and heavy-duty coolant tanks that had to be recharged and refrozen after each trip.

Helen picked her way between the crash-couches, rocking slightly with the motion of the treads until she emerged into the main corridor. Ben and Michael had gone ahead of her and already crowded behind Kevin's and Adrian's chairs in the command area. They all stared through the main window that wrapped around the scarab's nose.

The scarab ground its careful way across the nightside of Venus. Outside, the cracked surface of Ruskalia Planitia glowed with the heat it radiated, creating a quilt of deep reds, bright oranges, and clear, clean yellow. Overhead, the light reflected off the clouds, lending them the color and texture of molten gold being stirred by some invisible hand.

Kevin, a cautious, quiet man, who was almost twice as broad in the shoulders as his younger brother, kept his gaze flickering between the map displays and the window which showed them Beta Regio, a ragged wall of living fire wavering in the distance.

Coming down several kilometers from the whatever-it-was had seemed prudent. They did not want to land accidentally on something important.

As Beta Regio grew larger, the plain under the scarab's treads became rougher. Small, knife-backed ridges, blood red with escaping heat and blurred by the thick atmosphere, rose out of the plain. The closer they came to Beta Regio, the higher the ridges rose, until they became ragged walls. At last, Scarab Fourteen drove down a glowing corridor, following the path carved by a river of ancient lava.

A million similar paths spread out around the various Venusian highlands. Kevin drove the scarab gently over the rocks and swells, guided by the global positioning readout and the signals from his brother's drones.

The lava trail dead-ended at a sharp, smooth cliff that shone a livid orange. Some coal-bright sand rolled lazily along the brilliant ground, brushing against the hatchway set into the living rock.

"Venera Base," said Kevin in the general direction of the radio grill. "This is Scarab Fourteen." It was somehow comforting to see he was staring, as was Adrian. *As are we all.* "We have the . . . target in sight. Are you getting our picture?"

"We're getting it, Boss." Helen almost didn't recognize Charlotte Murray's voice, with its undertone of uncertainty, as if she were torn between fear and awe.

Helen understood the feeling. Her own eyes ached from staring at the brightly shining artifact. It was a perfectly circular shaft, about two meters across, that protruded half a meter out of the rugged surface. It glowed red hot, like its surroundings. Its lid had a series of, what?—handles? locks?— spaced evenly on all the sides she could see.

She glanced at Ben and saw his thoughts shining plainly on his face. It had to be a hatchway. It couldn't be anything else. Someone had built it there. That was the only explanation.

She knew he was not about to say any of that out loud, however. It wouldn't do. It was bad science and poor leadership, neither of which Ben would tolerate.

"Well"—she straightened up—"who's coming out to take a look?"

"Dr. Failia, you're not—" began Kevin. Helen silenced him with a glance. He was probably right. It probably was not a good idea for an eighty-something who was behind on her med trips to don a heavy hardsuit and go outside on Venus for a bit of a ramble.

But I'll be damned if I'm staying behind to watch this through the window.

"Right behind you, Helen," said Ben. Michael didn't say anything. He just headed down the narrow central corridor toward the changing area at the back of the scarab.

Helen rolled her eyes and followed, with Ben and Adrian filing after her. As copilot, Adrian's primary job was monitoring, or baby-sitting, any extravehicular activities. The EVA staging area took up most of the scarab's wide back end. Still, there somehow never seemed to be quite enough room for even three people to get into the bulky hardsuits.

The hardsuits themselves consisted of two layers. The soft, cloth-lined inner suit went directly over a person's clothes. This layer carried the coolants circulating in microtubules drawn from tanks which were pulled from the freezer and strapped, along with the O_2 packs, over the shoulders.

Then the pressure shell was assembled. Based on the hardsuits used in very deep industrial sea diving, it kept the user's personal pressure at a comfortable one atmosphere. It was also heavy as all get-out. Despite the internally powered skeletons, every time she put one on, Helen felt like a clunky monster from outer space.

But it was all necessary. The best simulations they had suggested that a person exposed to Venus's surface temperature and pressure would flash-burn a split second before any remaining chemical residue was squashed flat.

Finally, Helen locked down her helmet. The edges of the faceplate lit up with the various monitor readouts and the control icons. Helen had never liked the icons. They were line-of-sight controlled and she found them clumsy to use. Adrian looped the standard tool belt around her waist and stood back.

"Check one, check one, Dr. Failia." Adrian's voice came through her helmet's intercom. Following routine, Helen waved her hand in front of her suit's chest camera. "Reading you, Scarab Fourteen," she said. The monitors in each hard-suit were slaved to the scarab for earliest possible detection of mechanical trouble.

"And we have you, Dr. Failia," replied Adrian, glancing at the wall monitors. "Check two, check two, Dr. Godwin." The routine was repeated with Ben and Michael. Helen leaned against the wall and tried not to think too much about what waited outside. The picture had burned itself into her mind. It was an artificial structure, no question there. She couldn't wait until the rest of the solar system saw it. Good God, they'd say, there was somebody else out here or there had been. Her Venus, her beautiful, misunderstood twin to Earth, housed or had housed intelligent life. . . .

Steady Helen. Remember, you still don't know anything.

The checks on Ben's and Michael's suits came up green, and Adrian let them all move into the airlock. He swung the hatch shut behind them. The suits maintained pressure for their in-habitants, but the airlock had to equalize the pressure inside and outside before the hatch would open. That meant pumping the room up to a full ninety atmospheres worth of pressure.

As the pump started chugging, Ben turned toward Helen. "Well, it's either aliens or the biggest practical joke in human history."

"If we open it up and a bunch of those springy worms fly out, we'll know, right?" said Michael, carefully bending his knees to sit on a bench he couldn't quite see.

"Would they fly out, under pressure?" asked Helen. "Or would they just sort of pop and bounce?"

"That's one for Ned and the atmospherics people." Michael's hands moved restlessly, tapping against his thighs to some internal rhythm.

There seemed to be nothing else to say. Each of them lapsed into silence, thinking their own thoughts, making their own calculations or dreaming of their own futures. It took about fifteen minutes to pressurize the airlock. Right now, it felt like hours.

But finally the gauges all blinked green. Ben worked the levers on the outer hatch and swung it open.

"Good luck, Team Fourteen," came Adrian's voice.

One by one the governing board stepped out onto the glowing Venusian surface. Helen had never been so aware of being watched—monitored by her suit, overseen by Adrian and all Scarab Fourteen's cameras, followed by her colleagues, tracked by Derek's drones, which sat dormant on their own little treads, a short distance from the target object.

She took refuge in chatter. She activated the general intercom icon.

"Failia to Scarab Fourteen," she said. "Are you receiving?"

"Receiving loud and clear, Dr. Failia," answered Adrian. "Our readings say all suits green and go."

"All green and go out here," she returned. "Except Dr. Godwin forgot the marshmallows."

"That was on *your* to-do list, Helen," shot back Ben. Helen smiled. That had been an early experiment. The marshmallow exposed to the Venusian atmosphere had not roasted, however. It had scrunched up and vaporized. The egg they'd attempted to fry on the rock had exploded.

The memory spread a smile across Helen's face and made it easier to concentrate on the way in front of her. The cracks in the crust could be wide enough to catch a toe in, sending a person tumbling down in a most undignified fashion and wasting time while they were helped back to their feet—if their suit held up to the fall. If it didn't, there'd be nothing left to help up.

Helen dismissed that thought but held her pace in check with difficulty. She did not want to waste any more time. She wanted to sprint on ahead, but she had to settle for a slow march.

Still, they got steadily closer to the target. The closer they got, the more obvious it became that the object had to be artificial. It was indeed perfectly circular. The smooth sides rose about a half meter out of the rock. A series of smaller spheres protruded from it. For a moment, the three of them all lined up in front of the thing, examining it in reverent silence.

"Okay." The word came out of Michael like a sigh. "What's the procedure? Measure it first?"

"Measure it first," said Helen.

Slowly, Helen, Michael, and Ben circled the target in a strange, clumsy dance, recording everything yet again and measuring all of it. Yes, the drones had technically done all of this, but that was the machine record. This was the human record, and they needed it to help prove that this object was not just the result of some computer graphics and hocus-pocus.

The shaft was exactly forty-four centimeters in height and one and a half meters in diameter. A second, apparently separate section rested on or was attached to the top. That section was also one and a half meters in diameter but was only ten centimeters thick. Small, spherical protrusions, each appearing to be ten centimeters across, were attached to the sides of the upper section (like somebody'd stuck a half-dozen oranges there, Ben noted), equally spaced at sixty-degree intervals and attached by some undetermined means. A small circle, eight point three centimeters in diameter, had been inscribed three point six-four centimeters from the outer edge of the top section.

"Well, you're the expert, Ben," said Helen. "Is it or is it not naturally occurring?"

Ben's helmet turned toward her. "You're kidding, right, Helen?"

"No, I'm not." Helen remained immobile. "I want this all for the record."

"Okay, then." There came a brief shuffling noise that might have been Ben shrugging inside his suit. "In my opinion, based on the observations of the previous robotic investigation and my own two eyes, this is not a naturally occurring formation."

"To my knowledge, no one on Venera Base has ever authorized construction of such an object," added Helen.

"Are you going to open it, Helen, or can I go ahead?" Michael asked mildly.

Helen bit her lip. Part of her wanted to call down a whole team to swarm over the thing, analyzing every molecule before they did anything else. She told herself that was the good scientist part of herself. The truth was somewhat less flattering.

I'm afraid: of what we're doing, of what might, or might not, happen next.

"If you want to try, Michael, be my guest." Helen stepped back, hoping no one realized she was giving in to the private fear that bubbled, unwelcome, out of the back of her mind.

Michael walked around the hatch. He ran his fingers over the small circle set flush against the lid. He walked around the shaft again. Finally, he grasped two of the protrusions and leaned to the right.

The hatch slid slowly, unsteadily, sideways. A huge white cloud rushed out. Michael lurched backward.

"Steam?" said Ben incredulously. "There was water in there?" There was no water on the surface of Venus. Some particles in the clouds, but other than that, nothing.

"No analysis on that," came back Adrian. "Sorry."

"Not your fault," murmured Helen.

The cloud evaporated, and they all bent over the dark shaft. A tunnel sank straight into the bedrock. Their helmet lights shone on the bottom about four, maybe five, meters down. The first ten centimeters or so of rock around the mouth glowed brightly, but after that, it darkened to a shiny black, shot through with charcoal-gray veins. Thick staples had been shoved into the rock just below the glow-line, making what appeared to be the widely spaced rungs of a ladder.

Five sets of eyes stared. Three cameras recorded the ladder. One recorded the doctors as they waited. Nothing happened. Well, nothing new happened.

Helen straightened up and looked at her colleagues. Ben and Michael returned her gaze. She saw the awe tinged with ashamed fear in their eyes and felt a little better.

"All right, gentlemen," she said. "Let's go meet the neighbors."

One careful step at a time, she climbed down into the shaft.

What none of them saw, not with their cameras, not with their own eyes, was how one of the outcroppings on the side of Beta Regio crawled a little closer to the hatchway, as if to get a better look.

Chapter Two

The clouds of Home hung low overhead, pushing thick, yellow fingers deep into the clear. Harvest flies swarmed around them, feasting on spoiling algae or floater larvae. Here and there, a solitary shade darted into the swarm, skimmed off a few flies, and soared away.

There should be a thousand of them, thought T'sha as she watched the tiny bird. *Where have they all gone? Why are the flies winning?*

It was not just the absence of birds that disturbed the day. It was the smell, or the lack of it. The wind supporting her body blew light and sterile. It should have been heavy with salt, sweat, and rich, growing life. The dayside currents never blew empty from the living highlands. Except, today they did.

T'sha tilted her wings to slow her flight. This was not good. According to the reports, the winds had been reseeded with nutritive monocellulars not twelve miles from here. Had the seed been bad, or had the planting failed to take? Had they underestimated the imbalance on the microscopic layers here? If they had, what else had they underestimated?

It might be something else, whispered a treacherous voice in the back of her mind.

No, she chided herself. *I will not believe blasphemous rumors.*

People were not straining the winds right off the highlands to take fresh monocellulars for their homes. There had been patrols. They had found nothing. No one would be guilty of so much greed, so much sin. At least, not yet. Things had not gone so far yet.

At least, they shouldn't have. But winds that were empty of algaes and krills and other nutritional elements were becoming more common. Worse, there was word from the Polars that some of their winds were becoming currents of poison. A permanent migration down to the Rough Northerns was being debated even now if the Northerners could be persuaded to accept such a move.

Below T'sha spread the canopy, bright with its mottled golds, blues, and reds. From this distance, it looked healthy, ready for a casual single harvester or a concentrated reaping. But before too many more hours had passed, T'sha knew she was going to have to go down in there while the team confirmed what she suspected: that there would be too many flies down there too and not enough birds or puffs to clear them out. They would travel deep into the underside between the canopy and the crust and see the canopy's roots withering.

It was just as well the area itself was lightly traveled. She scanned the horizon in all directions and, apart from her own team, saw only one distant sail cluster. Her headset told her that it was the Village Gaith. T'sha reflexively gave orders to send greetings to the city and its speakers.

The rest of her team worked less than a half mile away. Their bright-white kites and stabilizers billowed in the sterile wind. T'sha could almost feel the engineers glancing nervously toward her. She was not behaving as she should. She was not a private person anymore. She was an ambassador to the High Law Meet. Her duties, in addition to making

promises on behalf of her city and representing her city to the
legislature and courts, included making people nervous. She
was supposed to be hovering around the edges of the team,
waiting for them to give her the words to carry back to the
Meet.

*Come now; time to play your part. You want the truth; you
need to go collect it.* T'sha banked, curving her path back toward her team. *You're doing no good drifting out here sniffing and brooding.*

A waver in the air currents over her shoulder made her
glance back. A new orange kite sailed on the wind. T'sha
turned in a tight circle to read the signal lights flashing on its
frame. Her bones bunched briefly.

What does D'seun want here?

Like T'sha, D'seun served as an ambassador to the High
Law Meet. She respected him as a close reasoner and an even-
minded legislator. His birth village had died when he was still
a child, but, against great odds, he had risen to become ambassador of his adopted city. She had wished many times they
did not hover on opposite sides of every debate concerning
the search for New Home. D'seun could only be here to check
up on her team. The samples they were analyzing would help
measure how critical the ecological breakdown here on Home
was and so help determine how much time they had to make
decisions regarding the new world.

She considered heading straight back to the survey team.
But then she decided that keeping D'seun at a distance from
her people might be advisable.

*Let them get as much done as possible without him flutter-
ing behind and making suggestions. The circumstances here
might not be as bad as they seem.*

T'sha fanned her wings, letting the wind proceed without
her and waiting for D'seun's kite to approach.

His kite was a pleasant hybrid with sails of orange skin and gold ligaments. Startling green scales dotted the shell-strip struts. Its engine was shut down, and it coasted on nothing more than the power of the wind. D'seun balanced half-inflated on the kite's perches. He raised both forehands in greeting to her.

T'sha spread her forehands in return. As D'seun and his kite drew near her, T'sha stilled her wings and let the wind pull her along so she could keep level with him.

"Good luck, Ambassador T'sha," he said pleasantly, shifting sideways to make room for her on the perches. "Will you join me?"

"Good luck, Ambassador D'seun. Certainly, I will." There was no disagreement between them so great that courtesy could be disregarded. T'sha cupped her wings to lift herself up slightly and wrapped all twenty-four fingers around the kite's perches. Then she deflated herself until her back and crest were level with D'seun's. They touched forehands formally.

D'seun was even younger than T'sha was. The bright gold of his skin sparkled strong and clear in the daylight, leaving his heavy maze of tattoos, both official and personal, in dark relief. His white and blue crest, which marked him as an Equatorial, streamed all the way down to his shoulderblades. T'sha suspected both the crest and the skin were enhanced. Fully inflated, he was only slightly smaller than she was, something T'sha was ashamed to admit she found disconcerting. Even her birth father was only three-quarters of her size.

D'seun spoke to the kite in its command language, softly ordering it to change its drift so they angled away from the survey team's distant sails. Disquiet gathered in the pockets between T'sha's bones.

"What brings you out here?" T'sha asked, deliberately keeping the question conversational.

"I had to call into the High Law Meet to finish some reportings." D'seun settled his weight back on his posthands, leaving his forehands free to stroke the kite's ligaments. "So I was there when the Seventh Team returned."

The Seventh? Oh, no. T'sha's mother had still been a child when ten worlds had been selected as candidates for New Home. T'sha had heard the memories of the raging debate as to whether Number Seven, which had . . . complications . . . , should be included in the roster of test worlds. Ambassador Tr'ena, one of T'sha's predecessors in the ambassadorship of Ca'aed, had lobbied hard against its inclusion. He had lost. T'sha had had to deal with the consequences of that loss.

D'seun, on the other hand, had risen to the rank of ambassador on the strength of what he and the Seventh Team had accomplished on that same world.

D'seun turned his gaze from the kite's ligaments. "The seedings have taken on their candidate. The life base is spreading. We have found New Home."

"They have taken on this candidate." T'sha pushed her muzzle forward. "What about the others?"

D'seun swelled, as if he carried the best of news. "None of the other seedings were successful. It is Number Seven, or it is nothing."

"There are other worlds out there. Millions of them."

"We do not have the time to test those millions."

T'sha strained the wind through her teeth. It held nothing, no taste, no texture, no scent. Empty air. Good for nothing but carrying flies and bad news.

"You came all this way to tell me this? You could have sent a message. I do wear a radio." She tapped the fine neural mesh of her headset for emphasis.

T'sha searched D'seun's stance and bearing, trying to get some feel for what he wanted. Despite his confident size, he was not at ease. He gripped and released the perches with each hand in turn so that he rocked unsteadily. His eyes darted about behind their lenses, looking for something other than her.

"There are things I wished to say to you directly," said D'seun blandly.

T'sha's posthands clenched the perch a little more tightly. "What are they? Do not speak against this candidate world? Do not say that if we must take this candidate, we must approach the New People and tell them plainly what we have come to New Home to do?"

D'seun inflated himself a little bit more. "The Seventh is the only planet where the life base has taken." Light sparkled against his skin and his tattoos. He had several new patterns running down his shoulder—a kite with billowing sails, a pattern of interlinking diamonds, and an ancient pictorial symbol for movement.

T'sha turned her gaze from D'seun's personal vanity. "Did the Seventh Team also report that the activities of the New People are increasing?" Her friend Pe'sen had monitor duty at the Conoi portal cluster. Now and then, he slipped her advance notice of team reports.

"That's all to the good," said D'seun calmly.

"Is it?" T'sha watched the cloud fingers in front of them with their haze of flies. Perhaps some hunter birds could be imported from the higher latitudes. They adapted well and needed little breeding supervision.

"What else could it be? Life must expand. Life helps life." The intensity of his words rippled the air. She could feel them against the skin of her muzzle.

Is that what you believe? Or are you only saying that because you know it's what I believe? With D'seun, this could be a question. She had seen him use partial truths to manipulate speakers and ambassadors before.

"Not all life views the world, perhaps I should say worlds, in the same way." T'sha pointed her muzzle toward the thick, sulfurous columns of haze and rot. "We see this abundance of flies as a danger signal. How do the flies see it?"

D'seun held up one forehand. "Intelligent life understands the void must be filled." That was an old truism, one that had never been put to the test. D'seun knew that as well as T'sha did.

"But filled with what?" muttered T'sha.

D'seun deflated until he was level with her again. "It is a question, certainly."

"No, it is *the* question," said T'sha. "And it is the one we are not asking."

She watched the bones under his skin expand and contract as he resisted the urge to swell up and tower over her. "*You* certainly are."

"Because someone must." She had carefully gone over all the available memories of the New People. They themselves were as hard to see as shellfish in their shells, but their creations were easily found. Their creations existed on three planets and one satellite of the Seventh World system, and one of those planets was Seventh World itself.

What did not seem to exist was any sign of life outside the shells, which was what breathed life into the debates. No good information had yet been acquired about their home world. They were obviously intelligent, but if they were not actively spreading life to New Home, were they making legitimate use of its resources? And if they were not making legitimate use of its resources, what stopped the People from doing so? There were those who argued that a system that already supported life was the best place to move themselves to. It would provide community, knowledge, and resources. D'seun was one of those, although he generally argued much more about knowledge and resources than he did about community.

Until now, of course.

D'seun deflated, becoming small, tight, and hard. "We need a new haven and new resources to ride out this imbalance." He sounded like a recording, running over and over until the feel of his words overwhelmed his audience and they could draw in nothing else.

Remain calm. Remain calm. You are an ambassador now and do not have the luxury of unchallenged opinion. T'sha leaned closer, seeking to draw him out. "Have you considered that contact with the New People will put an end to many questions?"

D'seun inflated slightly. "I agree, but this is not the right time. We must establish life beyond a few building blocks. We must be able to prove to the New People that we are serious about assisting with life's common goals."

Are you just trying this out on me? Why aren't you presenting this to the debate clusters? "But do we know they are common goals? Do we know the New People see things as we do?"

D'seun rippled his wings. "You and yours are too afraid of this thing we do. This is not greed. We need a new home, one where we can organize and arrange the life which supports us, where we can wait out what is happening on this old home of ours."

"I do not accuse you of greed," said T'sha. *Not yet.* "But you are right. Those I support act from fear. I am as afraid of taking this action as you and yours are afraid of not taking it." She leaned a little closer, her muzzle almost touching his. She wanted every word to sink into him. "Fear fills the air around you until you cannot feel what is truly happening to you." She pulled back and let herself swell until she felt her bones press hard against her skin. "We are all afraid. That is why we must question everything we do. We must act on our fear, but we must not act out of fear."

D'seun ruffled his bright crest, raising and spreading its

tendrils. "I feel your words. Do not think I am numb. But raising yet more uncertainty at this time could be disastrous. We must be sure, all of us."

T'sha looked down at him. He did not flinch or subside. He just returned her gaze.

At last, she asked, "What do you want?"

"I want to poll your city and its families. I have made a formal request to the High Law Meet. It will be sent to you within the hour."

T'sha's bones trembled. *I should have known this was coming. I should have read it in the way that flies are clustering.* "You question my fitness as ambassador?"

"No." D'seun's reply was easy, simple, and T'sha didn't believe it for a moment. "I seek to eliminate uncertainty in this great project we are undertaking. If your doubts truly reflect the doubts of your families, then it must be widely known."

Anger swelled T'sha until she thought she would float away on the wind. "Then let us set the polling time. But I tell you, D'seun"—she leaned close, making sure every word touched him—"I will not be stilled."

"Neither will the project, T'sha."

Whatever else he had been about to say was cut off by the voice of T'sha's headset vibrating through her ear. "Ambassador T'sha, this is Village Gaith. Help. You must help. I am in rot. You must help my people."

T'sha's wings spread in instant response. "We will be there."

"What's happening?" demanded D'seun.

"Village Gaith. It says it's in rot." She barked a quick transfer command to her headset. "Engineer K'taan!" she shouted for her team leader. "We have an emergency in Village Gaith. They are in rot. Take a sighting and get everyone there as quickly as you can."

Under the sound of her own voice, she heard D'seun give

orders to the kite. It unfurled its wings to their fullest extent and reined in its tail. The winds swept it up. Its engines added speed. T'sha made herself compact so as not to add any drag that might slow them down. The wind grew hard and full as it raced across her shoulders, pressing the kite into swift motion.

Another rot. How many did that make since the First Mountain last saw the dayside? How many cities in how many latitudes were dead or dying, and what was the total refugee count? Two and a half million? Had it gotten up to three million yet?

She spoke to her headset, telling it to seek details about Village Gaith. After a few moments, the set murmured back to her.

"Gaith is a Calm Northerns village, with about a thousand individuals from four different families calling it home. Sixty percent of the individuals are children. Individuals are good engineers, have contributed several widely adapted adjustments to canopy balance in recent years, and have raised several excellent surveyors and samplers. Its ambassador is T'nain V'gan Kan Gaith. He has been notified of the emergency at the High Law Meet and is returning now. Its local speaker is T'gai Doth Kan Gaith."

T'gai. Oh, memory. I haven't seen you since I was declared an adult. She remembered T'gai's visits to her parents' complex, his dark-gold skin, and his speaker's tattoos branching out all around his muzzle. He always had some new point of discussion to raise, some new poll to try to start. He was all a speaker ought to be—busy, serious, forward thinking.

How did a rot start in his own village?

She shook herself out of her own thoughts as she realized D'seun was watching her.

"I'm sorry. You spoke?"

D'seun dipped his muzzle. "I was saying this is your latitude. You should warn the cities."

Good, good. Pay attention, T'sha. There's work to do. "Yes. Of course." She commanded her headset to call Ca'aed.

"I hear you, Ambassador," returned her city's deep voice.

"Ca'aed, there's an emergency in Village Gaith. Warn the downwind cities to take quarantine precautions. I'm on my way to assess the damage. I'll have more news soon."

Even as she spoke the words, a fresh finger of wind touched her. This one was not empty. It was thick with something far too cloying to be a healthy scent. She could see Gaith in the distance—a sphere bristling with sails and sensor fronds. It looked peaceful, but that smell, that too sweet taste . . .

"I have their location, Ambassador. . . ." Ca'aed paused, and worry stiffened T'sha's bones. "I can't raise the village. I hear no voice."

T'sha glanced at D'seun, but he was looking straight ahead at Gaith. It took T'sha's eyes a moment to focus, but then she too saw what was wrong.

Around even the smallest village, there would be a few citizens flying freely about their business, but Gaith was surrounded by a swarm of its own people. They fluttered about the shell and bones like flies without purpose.

It was the sight of panic.

D'seun spoke to the kite. It brought them around to Gaith's windward side. They closed on the village, and T'sha saw that its sails and wind guides were no longer white, as they should have been. Huge patches of grayish-brown funguslike growths disfigured their surfaces.

The smell of rotting flesh engulfed her. T'sha instantly tightened in on herself. *Breath of life, bones of mine, what is happening here? I've never seen one this bad!*

The village cried as if hurt just by the wind of her approach. All around those diseased sails flew its citizens. Now they were close enough that T'sha could hear their voices—shouting, crying, demanding, trying to give orders. Above it all, she heard the wordless keening of the village's pain. It was dying and it did not know how to save itself. In its fear, it called desperately for its people.

D'seun snatched the bulky caretaker unit from out of the kite's holder and launched himself into the air. T'sha dipped her muzzle. The caretaker might be able to speak to the village where a person could not.

"Engineer K'taan," T'sha bawled into her headset as she launched herself into the air. "Where are you?"

"Approaching from leeward. We have you in sight."

"Get a catchskin under the village. We can't let the rot fall into the canopy!"

"Yes, Ambassador!"

Flies clustered everywhere, the eternal flies that should have been clustered around the clouds. The insects scattered in angry swarms around her wings. The smell was unbearable. T'sha closed her muzzle tightly and tried not to think of what was filtering in through her skin.

Bubbling gray fungus turned the nearest sails slick. Even as she watched, great patches melted and sagged. Speckled liquid ran down what was left of the clean white skin. Something unseen whimpered.

"Gaith! Gaith!" T'sha called through her headset. "Answer me! Are you there?"

No answer. None at all.

D'seun flew straight into the thickest crowd and started forming them up into an orderly flight chain. As soon as the formation was spotted, people started flocking toward it, leaving fewer to flap in panic around the dying village.

T'sha ordered her headset onto a general-call frequency. "This is T'sha So Br'ei Taith Kan Ca'aed, ambassador for

Ca'aed, to anyone who can hear me. I need Speaker T'gai Doth Kan Gaith at the center of leeward."

She got no answer. It was possible there was nothing healthy enough left to hear the call.

Ten yards below the city, K'taan directed a group of four researchers to stretch out the transluscent, life-tight catchsheet. It wasn't big enough. Two other researchers rushed in, carrying an additional sheet. They sealed the sheets together and spread them again. That was just enough if the wind did not take too much. They needed to get a quarantine blanket around the village as soon as possible. Why were those not grown generally?

Why is this happening at all?

"Ambassador T'sha."

T'sha wheeled on her wingtip. Behind her floated T'gai. His tattoos branched all the way to the roots of his crest now, but the crest was dimmed by age.

"Speaker T'gai." T'sha touched his forehands. "Good luck to you."

"Good luck to you, T'sha. Ambassador T'sha." His crest ruffled softly.

She tried not to feel the weakness in his words. "Why didn't you report this?" she asked as gently as she could.

"We thought . . . we thought . . ."

We thought we could take care of it. T'sha dipped her muzzle to let him know she understood. No people wanted to believe they could fail their city, or even their village. No one wanted the shame of having to make promises because they were not skilled enough or rich enough to care for their own, so they struggled in their silence until it was too late.

There were always dangers, particularly in the smaller villages such as Gaith, that drifted on their own rather than following in the wake of a larger, older city. Cortices got too closely bred and became unable to cognate as required.

Builders and assessors went insane and undid the work they were supposed to enhance. Corals used too many times without enough interior variety bleached in thin winds. Cancers took hold of the village's bones.

But now, infections were spreading around the world. A fungus or a yeast that should have been easy for an engineer to excise would instead burn through a city, breaking down everything it touched, sometimes turning from the city and attacking the people.

Even so, that usually took weeks. This . . . T'sha didn't dare let that thought go any further.

"We'll talk about that later." T'sha turned her mind to the problem. "I'm here with Ambassador D'seun and my survey team. We'll send some of them for kites and other transports. There are several healthy cities traveling this stream. But first you need to assemble your people. We'll need to have you checked out to make sure you are carrying nothing infectious." *We cannot let this spread. We dare not.*

T'gai withered. "We must tend our village. . . ."

T'sha swelled gently, trying to calm him with her authority. It felt strange. He was so much her senior in years. But now, she outranked him, and she must not shrink from that. "It has gone too far for that, Speaker. We need to quarantine Gaith. You must call in all the promises you have owing and divert them to diagnosis and prevention. Your ambassador will need all your help with that when he returns."

Speaker T'gai dipped his muzzle. "Yes, of course, Ambassador. You are right."

"Good." She glanced around. The catchsheet was stabilized and anchored to the village's sail struts. Someone had released a slurry of inch-long cleaners onto the sails. They slithered across the sails' skin, ingesting the bubbling growths until the toxicity became too much and they dropped onto the catchsheet. The skin left behind was almost transparent. Even as T'sha watched, the wind tore through the skin, leaving the sail in tatters. The sail mewled and tried to draw in on itself.

She pulled her gaze away. D'suen had a great line of people gathered in the orderly chain now. That would be where T'gai could help.

"Find your teachers to keep gathering your people together. Bring your engineers and doctors. We must determine what's gotten out and how far it's gone."

"Yes. Yes." The speaker swelled again to the lines and proportions she knew. "Thank you, Ambassador."

T'sha deflated until she was just a little smaller than T'gai. "With you, I am still just T'sha, Speaker T'gai." She returned to her normal size. "Go. We will do what we can."

As she watched T'gai fly away, she tried to enumerate what needed to be done. *We need a quarantine blanket. We need a team to find what cortices are still working. A way to repel these flies. . . .*

Life gone insane. Life taking more than it needed, swinging from balance into chaos. T'sha circled until she was upwind of the stench and the sounds of pain. The canopy was lush underneath them. The wind had good weight and texture. This rot seemed to be interested in animal materials; maybe at least the plants below would be safe.

T'sha tensed her bones. They could assume nothing. She'd have to go down and look. If the rot had gotten down there, they would probably be forced to cut it out. That made for a wasteful, inelegant cure, especially with so much of the canopy dying on its own, but they couldn't risk this getting carried any further.

Who knew what spores were already in the wind? Was this even really a fungus, or was she being fooled by appearances? T'sha shivered. On top of it all, here were a thousand more refugees. Some healthy cities would probably still take them in, but they would also demand hefty promissory obligations against the time Gaith, or a replacement, could be regrown. The children huddling under their parents' bellies would be declared adults before the village was free of its debts.

In an earlier time, some of the adults certainly would have offered to bind themselves into lifetime slavery to individuals who could help their children, but that was a practice that had been out of favor for at least two hundred years. Most teachers said accepting such a promise came very close to actual greed. Looking on this sight, T'sha was grateful.

But what sort of promises would T'gai be able to obtain for his people? They were good engineers, but if too many of them had to be indentured away to serve other cities, they would never be able to resurrect their village. They would become permanently homeless, scrabbling for their right to stay wherever they could find space, maybe permanently deprived of their votes.

"I've sent word of our situation to the High Law Meet." D'seun dropped into T'sha's line of sight.

T'sha shook her wings. "There isn't much to report yet."

"Not much to report!" D'seun bobbed up and down as if the sheer force of his exclamation rocked him. "Gaith is dead and decaying in front of our eyes! We have to spread the word!"

"Until we have a cause, that will do nothing but raise a panic." T'sha stopped. "Which is the idea, isn't it?" she murmured. "If the Law Meet panics, they will approve your candidate world without debate, won't they?"

"How can you even be thinking of debate?" demanded D'seun. "Surely this shows us there is no more time. We must make New Home ours or we will all die!"

A dozen different thoughts, realizations, and responses rippled through T'sha. But all she said was, "You and my engineers have the situation under care. I must return to Ca'aed to make sure the latitude quarantines are coordinated. May I borrow your kite?"

It was not a request he could easily refuse. "I will ask for a promise against this."

"A proportionate one, I'm certain."

T'sha found the required wind and flew back to the place where D'seun's kite waited. She gave it orders with the most urgent modifiers. The kite unfurled its wings without hesitation. Its engines sang as the air forced through them. T'sha flattened herself against the perches, wishing the team had brought a dirigible instead. But no need had been seen, no emergency anticipated. Certainly nothing like this.

The memories of the gray, bubbling growths coating Gaith's sails and the black ashlike substance clinging to its walls flew round and round inside T'sha's mind and she could not banish them.

D'seun had been a little right. This was new and this was deadly. The High Law Meet did have to be told. But told what? Told how? That was the next question.

The kite chattered in command language, sending the message on ahead that they were on an emergency run and traffic should clear the gates. Everything had some task to keep them busy, but not T'sha. All she could do was hang on until they reached the walls of Ca'aed.

The kite kept to the clearest routes. T'sha saw dirigibles and other kites in the distance, but did not ask any to be hailed. Even further away she saw the sails and walls of the Ca'aed's wake-villages. The villages saw her as well, and their voices began to pour through her headset.

"I've heard the message of Gaith. My speakers are on the alert. All precautions are being taken." This was T'aide, a young and confident village, strong in its faith of its people. "Good luck, Ambassador."

"Message received from Gaith. The diagnostics are roused." P'teri, an ancient village that had spread its boundaries so far there was talk of it growing into its own city.

P'teri was cautious and content, though, and had so far been unwilling to agree to the expansion. "Good luck, Ambassador."

Terse, protective T'zem came through next. "My people are well. I will keep them so. Look to Ca'aed, Ambassador."

I do. You may be sure that I do.

Ca'aed itself shimmered in the distance now, its breadth dominating the horizon. Kites, dirigibles, and people swarmed around it like flies. No, no, not like flies. Like hunter birds, like shades, or even puffs. Ca'aed would not fall to the flies.

Ca'aed was an ancient city. It's pass-throughs, arches, sails, and gardens had grown huge and richly colored with age. Its highest sails nearly raked the clouds, and its sensor roots dragged in the canopy. Where villages skimmed and bobbed on the winds, Ca'aed sailed ponderous and stately, as if it graciously allowed the winds to carry it along.

T'sha's family had helped the city grow its shells and sails. They had protected it and been protected by it for thirty generations. They had been pollers, speakers, teachers, engineers, and ambassadors. Always, always, they had worked directly with Ca'aed, heard its voice, helped it live.

No, Ca'aed would not fall.

Ca'aed spread like a person fully inflated with their wings flung wide. Its walls were deeply creviced, making a thousand harbors into which to guide its people or their vehicles. It drew people in and exuded them again, as if people were what it breathed. Its lens eyes sparkled silver in the daylight. It watched the people come and go so it could advise them as to their routes and their loads or simply to wish them good luck. Lacy fronds of sensors stretched between the sails, constantly testing the winds, looking for riches to steer into and disease to steer away from. Ca'aed was careful. Ca'aed was well advised. Ca'aed might act quickly but never rashly.

"No wonder you have no husbands yet," her younger sister T'kel had teased her once. "Your love is all for the city."

"That is no bad thing," her birth father had replied. "If someone in the position to make promises does not love the city as well as she loves the people in it, she may grow careless with her promises and perhaps overtax its capacities. This can force growth where growth is not ready or even advisable." He'd been answering T'kel, but his attention had been on T'sha. That had been while she was being debated in the general polls as a speaker, but already her father was trying to convince her to start building a base to become ambassador.

"Welcome home, Ambassador," came Ca'aed's familiar voice from her headset. "Have you answers from Gaith? Is there a name for its illness?"

"We don't know yet." All T'sha's hands clutched the perches uneasily.

"But you are confident it will be found?"

"Not as confident as I was." T'sha deflated just a little. "I have to send the kite back to Gaith. Open your gates for me?"

"Always, T'sha. Give me your kite."

T'sha spoke the words to transfer command and Ca'aed took over, pulling the little kite unerringly into one of its harbors. As the rich brown walls surrounded them, Ca'aed's welcomers fluttered out of their cubbyhole and surrounded T'sha in a swarm of reds and greens. They lighted here and there on her back and wings, tasting the emissions of her pores and flitting away again for Ca'aed to be sure there were no dangerous tastes, that she carried nothing hidden with her from Gaith.

But nothing was found, and the pebbled gates at the end of the harbor, which constantly strained and tested the winds for the beneficial elements as well as for the harmful ones, opened a portal for her to dart through. One of Ca'aed's fronds brushed her as she passed, a touch of reassurance and welcome.

"An old city," her birth father had often said, "becomes as full, rich, and complex as the canopy underneath, and its life becomes as tightly intertwined."

T'sha sometimes thought "tangled" would be a better word. The inside of Ca'aed was decidedly a tangle. Bones braced it, corals defined its spaces, and ligaments bound its elements together. Plants and animals gave its walls color, and its air weight and life.

Between them, Ca'aed was a shell full of shells. Small dwellings and family compounds were tethered to each other and to the city, but were not part of its essential substance.

Ca'aed's free citizens flew through its chambers, intent on their various businesses, or merely enjoying the tastes and textures of their world. Its indentured worked down in the veins and chasms of its corals, growing, researching, comparing, because the city could not be wholly aware of the workings of every symbiont and parasite, any more than a person could be aware of the workings of every pore.

Music, perfumes, voices, flavors filled the air, vying for attention, pressing against T'sha's skin, filling her up with the vigor of life. The memory of Gaith made the miasma all the more precious. The people of Gaith had lost all of this when they lost their village. But, with care, T'sha might still be able to help them get it back.

T'sha flew into the tangle of life, angling herself vaguely toward her family's district. "Ca'aed, I need my brother T'deu. Where is he?"

"Your brother is in the promise trees."

Of course. T'sha beat her wings, turning her flight up toward the city's sculpted and vented ceiling. The promise trees were in this finger of the city. She would not have to snag a passing kite.

A solid turquoise and cream carapace encapsulated the promise trees and kept out not only the winds but all that the winds might carry. The ligaments that twined around its oval walls and anchored it to Ca'aed's living bones did not themselves live. They carried neither information nor nutrition and so could not be used to tamper with anything within the carapace.

The only entrance to the trees was a long tunnel that was so narrow that only one person at a time could fly its length. Pink and gold papillae tasted the air around each entrant, making sure that he or she was a free citizen of Ca'aed. If the entrant was a stranger to the city or an indenture, it made sure he or she had received permission from the city or a speaker to come. If not, the ends of the tunnel would seal and Ca'aed would call for the district's speaker.

Entering the trees was like flying straight into the canopy. It was a jungle of leaves, stems, branches, and trunks, all grown into one another. They spread from the center of the room to the carapace. They climbed the walls, until patterns of intertwining stems and roots covered the carapace's grainy hide. All the colors of growing life shone there in a delicate riot. It all appeared extremely fragile, but the slightest root was many times stronger than the thickest metal wire T'sha had ever touched. It was as beautiful to T'sha as any temple.

Inside the trees' veins flowed the DNA records of every registered promise of the world of Home. Not all promises were registered. Promises passed every day between friends and family that had no need to be here, but promises between businesses, between cities and villages, between ambassadors and any person or any city needed to be recorded. Their fine tendrils of implication needed to be tracked. In here were promises of marriage, merger, birth, inheritance, indenture, trade, service, and sale.

None of this luxuriant growth was necessary, of course. All

of the promise registries could have been contained in a set of
cortex boxes, and in a younger city it might have been, but the
beauty and elaboration of Ca'aed was one of the aspects of it
that T'sha had always loved about her city.

T'deu, T'sha's older brother, hovered near the top of the
chamber, away from the other trackers and registrants who
dotted the chamber. T'deu was an archiver, trained in the
reading and tracking of promises. T'sha wove her way
through the maze of stems and branches until the air of her
passage brushed against him. Her brother turned on his
wingtip and leaned forward, rubbing his muzzle joyfully
against hers.

"Ambassador Sister!" he said, softly but happily. She and
T'deu shared the same birth mother. His father had entered
the marriage because of a political promise, and hers had been
promised in to help his family when their city fell into trouble. She and T'deu had been raised together and never lost
their friendship, even after they were both declared adults and
sent out to make their own lives. "It is good to have you here,
no matter what the circumstances."

"Thank you, Archiver Brother." T'sha pulled away just a
little. "You heard about Gaith."

He dipped his muzzle. "Ca'aed spread the word to the
speakers, and the speakers have not been silent."

T'sha's bones bunched as she winced, but she smoothed
them out. "Brother, we need to redirect this wind. It is going
to be used to rush us into an untenable situation."

T'deu peered up at her, as if he could see into her mind and
touch her thoughts. "If you tell me so," he said, but he did not
sound certain.

T'sha accepted his words and dismissed his tone. "I want
us to bring Gaith's body here."

Her brother deflated in a long, slow motion. "That's dangerous, T'sha—"

"No, listen, there are advantages here. If we give Gaith's engineers the resources to regenerate and resurrect the city and they give us the knowledge and experience they gain from the task, we will be able to turn around and make our own promises with that information, should this strain of disease spread."

"It will mean bringing in a potential contagion, though," T'deu reminded her. "You'll have to take a vote on that."

"I'll get the votes. Can you design me a promise that will do the job?"

"I can design anything you like." T'deu waved one wing at the maze of stems and branches around them. "I could grow you a tree that would outline ownership of the clouds above us. Implementing it—"

"Is my job," said T'sha, cutting him off. "Make sure you graft P'kan's engineers into its branches. They hold several promises against the city. This will help close those down."

"Of course, Ambassador," T'deu said, deflating with mock servility. "Anything else?"

"Should fresh thoughts sprout, I'll share them with you."

T'deu moved even closer, making sure his words reached only her. "Why are you really doing this, Ambassador Sister? It is not only for the profit of the city, or even for the good of Gaith."

"No," she admitted. For a moment she thought of telling him he did not need to know, but that was not true. To design a truly effective promise, he needed to know the ultimate goal, especially if the promise were complex, as promises dealing with cities ultimately were. Trying to integrate the wrong person could jeopardize the entire balance. "I want to be sure Gaith is studied, and studied immediately. If I leave it free for D'seun to take over, he'll fly the village's bones all around the world and show everyone what horrors we are exposing ourselves to if we don't all flock to New Home immediately."

"He'll still try to use Gaith's illness to overfly you," said T'deu.

T'sha shook her wings. "I won't let him. All D'seun's attention is fixed on a single point. If he will not voluntarily see the whole horizon, he must be made to see."

T'deu dipped his muzzle again. "As my Ambassador Sister says. I'll start growing your promise."

"Thank you, Brother. Good luck." She brushed her muzzle against his briefly and launched herself back toward the entrance.

And now there are only a thousand meetings to arrange. The district speakers must hear all of this of course and be brought around. That could be expensive. I'll have to organize the pollers for a citywide referendum, but their schedule should be light right now, except for the poll D'seun has so thoughtfully called for. T'sha emerged from the tunnel into the filtered light of the city. She turned her flight toward the city center and her family's district where she kept her workspace. "Ca'aed?"

"Yes, Ambassador?" answered the city.

"Ca'aed, I have a case to put to you. It concerns your wellbeing, so I cannot move without you."

"What is it?"

As T'sha flew, she told Ca'aed her plan to bring Gaith to the city to allow Gaith's own citizens to effect its resurrection in return for sharing their knowledge with Ca'aed's engineers, thus saving the Kan Gaith years of potential indenture for their food and shelter in some other city.

Ca'aed was silent for a moment. "We have the room to bring the Kan Gaith here," it said finally. "Our binding of promises with them is not strong or detailed, but there is some exchange that could be worked out." Again, the city paused.

T'sha suspected it was mulling over the conversation T'sha had held with T'deu. "We do need to know what infects Gaith," Ca'aed went on. "Yes, bring it here. I agree. I will start working on precautionary plans so we can implement this action as soon as you have secured the people's votes."

"Thank you, Ca'aed," said T'sha earnestly. "This is not just to further my cause with the High Law Meet. There is good for all concerned here."

"Yes," answered Ca'aed. "I do comprehend the good in this."

Something in the city's voice kept T'sha from asking what else it comprehended.

T'sha's workspace was a small coral bubble in her family's compound. The veins holding her records twined all around its insides, spreading out crooked tendrils of blue and purple. It was not as grand or complex a space as many ambassadors had, but T'sha preferred to work on the wing and conduct her meetings and requests in person.

This time though, that would be impossible. She needed all of her specially trained cortex boxes to organize a meeting of the city's thirty district speakers and coordinate their schedules. Each speaker, in turn, would have to reserve time with their chiefs and the pollers because this was a voting matter. The entire process would take dodec-hours.

T'sha was not even halfway finished when the room told her D'seun waited outside.

"Let him in," she said, reluctantly. She was not quite ready for him yet, but she had no polite way to delay.

D'seun drifted into her workspace. He looked shriveled and settled at once on a perch.

"Good luck, D'seun. Can I offer you some time in the refresher? Surely whatever you have to say can wait an hour or two until you are restored."

"No, it cannot wait." He lifted his muzzle. "I must hear you say that you now understand that we cannot wait to find another world to be New Home. I must hear you say we will work together in this."

Shock swelled T'sha. That really was all he thought about. There was no swaying him, no changing the focus of his mind.

"I understand that we are not always as wise as we think we are," she told him fiercely, leaning forward from her own perch. "I understand that we might not know all the rules of life, and that if we act like we do, we are breeding disaster, for ourselves and for these New People."

"I respect your caution, Ambassador T'sha, but I cannot let it endanger us any further." Righteousness swelled D'seun to his fullest extent. "I will proceed with the poll of your families."

"I know that," replied T'sha calmly. "I'm already arranging time with the speakers and the pollers. You will have your vote."

D'seun cocked his head. His eyes examined her from crest to fingertip, trying to guess what made her so complacent. If he succeeded, he gave no sign. "Thank you for your cooperation then, Ambassador. I will wish you good luck and go prepare for the vote."

"Good luck, Ambassador D'seun." T'sha lifted her hands. D'seun lifted his briefly in return and flew away.

T'sha watched him go. *There are advantages to dealing with someone whose attention has narrowed to a hairsbreadth*, she thought. *He has not yet thought to make a try for Gaith's body.*

"Ambassador?" came Ca'aed's voice suddenly.

"Yes, Ca'aed?"

"I want you to know, I'm going to vote in favor of using D'seun's candidate for New Home."

"What?" T'sha stiffened. "Ca'aed, why?"

"Because I'm afraid, T'sha. I'm afraid that what happened to Gaith will happen to me and to you."

T'sha shriveled in on herself as the city's words washed through her. Ca'aed was afraid. She had never heard the city voice such a thought before. What could she do against that?

"We will protect you, Ca'aed," she murmured. "But who will protect the New People?"

"You will find a way."

T'sha dipped her muzzle. "I will have to."

CHAPTER THREE

"This is your 7 A.M. wake-up," said the room's too sweet voice. "This is your 7 A.M. wake-up."

Around Veronica, the hotel suite woke up. The lights lifted to full morning brightness. In the sitting room, the coffeemaker began to gurgle and hiss, while a fresh lemon scent wafted out of the air ducts.

Vee, who had been awake for an hour already, looked up, sniffed the combination of coffee and lemon, and wrinkled her nose.

"Should've shut off one of those," she muttered.

She looked back down at the desk screen in front of her with its list of names, degrees, and recent publications. She frowned for a moment and then moved Martha Pruess to the top of the list. She was a research fellow in photonic engineering from the Massachusetts Federated Institute of Technology, and her list of publications took up half the screen.

"Checking out the competition?"

Vee jumped, twisting in her seat. Rosa Cristobal, her friend and business manager, stood right behind her chair. "Jesus, Rosa. Don't sneak up on me. It's too early."

"Sorry." Rosa tucked her hands into the pockets of her thick, terry-cloth robe. "But that is what you're doing?"

"Yeah." Vee sighed and tugged on a lock of her hair. "Rosa, I am not going to get this."

"They invited you," Rosa pointed out, as patiently and as firmly as if this were the first time she'd said it.

"Why?" Vee spread her hands. "They need scientists, engineers. I'm an artist, for God's sake. It's been years since I've set foot in a real lab."

"You've got a Ph.D. in planetary atmospherics and your name is sitting pretty on five different patents."

"Which you will remind them of." Vee dropped her gaze back down to the list. *Actually, maybe Avram Elchohen should be at the top. He's got a few more papers on optoelectric engineering—*

"Which I will remind them of." Rosa reached over Vee's shoulder and touched the Off key. The desk screen blanked. "Get dressed, Vee. The interview's at nine and you do not want to be late."

"Yes, Rosa," said Vee in the tones of a child saying "Yes, Mommy." She got up meekly and headed for her bathroom. "And shut off the lemons, will you?"

"Yes, Vee."

After her shower, Vee dressed in an outfit she'd bought especially for the interview—wide navy-blue slacks and a matching vest with matte buttons over a sky-blue silk blouse. She stepped into the makeup station and selected a minimalist setting. The mirror glowed gently as it scanned her face and sent color instructions to the waldos, which responded by laying on just a hint of bronze to highlight her cheekbones and jawline, and a touch of deep wine to her lips.

"Close your eyes please," said the same too sweet voice that had given the wake-up call. Vee did and felt a quick puff of powder. She opened her eyes. Now her lids had a hint of burgundy coloring and a discreet sheen of gold dust glimmered on her cheeks, the very latest in conservo-chic.

"Routine complete," said the station.

Vee studied herself in the mirror for a minute. It was a good face, with high cheekbones, strong nose, soft chin. Her brows were so pale as to be almost nonexistent. The rest of her was what she called "Nordic swizzle-stick fashion," very long, very white, and very thin. "Handy for hiding behind flagpoles," she liked to joke.

Vee wound her mane of silver-blond hair into a tidy coil and pinned it in place. She selected a scarf that matched her blouse and fastened it so it covered her head but fluttered freely down over her shoulders. She nodded at her reflection, pleased. The effect was businesslike but not stuffy. It said that here was a person to be taken seriously.

Vee had been stunned when she saw the v-mail message from the Colonial Affairs Committee. She had sat in front of her living room view screen for ten full minutes, playing and replaying the recording.

"Hello, Dr. Hatch. I'm Edmund Waicek of the United Nations Colonial Affairs Committee Special Work Group on Venus."

Good breath-control exercise there, Vee remembered thinking, facetiously. Edmund Waicek was a tall man with red-brown skin and black eyes. A round, beaded cap covered his thick copper hair. His age was indeterminate and his clothing immaculate.

"As I am sure you are aware, there has been a remarkable discovery made on the world of Venus. We have found what appears to be the remains of an alien base or facility of some kind. Because of the vastly important nature of this development, the C.A.C. has decided to assemble a team of specialists to examine and evaluate the discovery." He leaned forward and flashed a smile full of carefully calculated sincerity. "We have reviewed your academic record and subsequent accomplishments, and we would like to invite you to participate in the interview process to see if you can take your place on this historic mission." His expression grew solemn. "We will need your answer by Tuesday the eighteenth at 9 A.M., your local time. Thank you for your attention to this matter. I look forward to meeting you."

The Discovery on Venus. Of course Vee had heard of it. It was a solid indication that there had once been alien life inside the solar system, an idea that had been given up on years before Vee had even been born. When she was feeling cynical, she would tell herself it was nothing more than three holes in the ground. Except it was. It was three holes in the ground dug by nothing human, and they had left behind what everyone was certain was a laser, or maybe it was a laser component of a larger machine.

It was that laser they wanted her to go up and take a look at. Well, they wanted someone to go up and take a look at it, and her name, somehow, had made the short list.

Veronica Hatch, science popularizer, temperamental artiste, and noted personality. The U.N. was setting all that aside and going back to the part of her that was Dr. Hatch, the part that had patents and papers and could do actual work.

"Vee?" came Rosa's voice.

Vee realized she hadn't moved. She was just standing there, staring at the reflection of a serious, competent stranger, and clenching her fists.

"Coming." Vee smoothed out her veil and turned away from the mirror.

Rosa was in the sitting room, drinking what was probably her second cup of coffee. How she could suck that stuff down on an empty stomach Vee had never known. Rosa had selected a tunic and skirt suit in shades of forest green with emerald trim and a pale, silver scarf to cover her black hair.

She looked Vee up and down and gave a small nod of approval as Vee twirled on her toes to show herself off.

"Very nice." Rosa drained her mug. "Do you want to order in, or go out for breakfast?"

"Would you mind if we dropped by the Coral Sea? I promised Nikki."

Rosa made a face. "That place is overdone."

"Hey." Vee drew herself up indignantly. "I helped design the effects on that place, thank you very much."

"And you overdid it." Rosa stood up. "In your usual stylish, trend-setting way." She grabbed her briefcase off the couch. "Let's hit the deck, shall we?"

Vee and Rosa took a glide-walk up through the layers of the Ashecroft Hotel to the main pedestrian deck and the clean, clear, Pacific day. U.N. City had been built during the first decade of what some people still called the Takeover. The Takeover happened halfway through the 2100s, when the United Nations went from being a pack of squabbling diplomats to a genuine world-governing body. Because national feeling still ran very high back then, it was decided that the seat of world government would not be given to any one country. It would float around the world on the oceans. The mobility created some trouble with time zones, but that was deemed a minor problem compared to the endless bickering caused by the debate over where to put the capital of the world.

The city itself was huge. Toward its center, you couldn't even tell you were on the ocean. Ashecroft was in the fashionable edge district however, and the first thing Vee saw when they emerged was sunlight sparkling cheerfully on the broad, blue Pacific. In the distance she could just make out three of the cordon ships that sailed in a ring around the city, serving as escort and border guard.

On the main deck, U.N. City was wide awake and in full

swing. Crowds of people swarmed between the buildings and the parks. Their skins were every color, from snow white to midnight black. They wore all styles and colors of clothing and every possible level of body enhancement, both organic and mechanical. Some drifted between the boutiques, studying the holo-displays that took the place of windows. Some strolled along the city's sculpted rail looking out at the calm, sapphire ocean, maybe hoping to see dolphins or, better yet, whales. Some just hurried from glide-walk mouth to glide-walk mouth, catching a few precious moments of sunlight between meetings and appointments down in the heart of the city.

How many of them are hustling to something related to the Venus Discovery? Vee felt a twinge of guilt at being happy for U.N. City's restrictive public assembly policies. You could barely move in Chicago without tripping over another "citizens meeting" or "public discussion" about Venus's underground chambers and their contents and what, if anything, should be done about them.

The Coral Sea Cafe was a few blocks from the railing, nestled in the corner between one of the observation towers and the Council of Tourism Welcome Center. The mirrored door scanned them both, found them admissible, and slid itself open. Vee stepped into the undersea-scaped interior with its wavery, water-scattered light, which she had fine-tuned for them. Schools of tropical fish swam lazily across the walls. The chairs and tables mimicked rounded stones or coral outcroppings.

"Just too-too," murmured Rosa. Vee slapped her shoulder.

A woman almost as tall and thin as Vee emerged from the office door, probably alerted to their arrival by the door. She looked like she was in her mid-twenties, but Vee knew she was using body-mod to keep middle age firmly at bay. Not even forty, Nikki had already waved her rights to children and signed up for long-life.

Nothing like knowing what you want.

A circle of blue glass shone in the middle of Nikki's forehead, probably concealing a personal scanner and database to let her know just who she was dealing with.

"Vee!" Nikki cried happily.

"Nikki!" Vee exclaimed, embracing the woman with the expected level of fervor. "Love the third eye. You look great."

"And you look"—Nikki pulled back just a little—"subdued."

"Ah." Vee held up one, long finger. "Someone's actually vetting me for a science job today."

Nikki's smile grew conspiratorial. "This is about the Venus thing, isn't it? I heard your name on the lists."

"Well surely, nothing important can happen without my name on it," announced Vee regally.

"Surely, dear, surely," said Nikki, grasping Vee's hand.

Rosa coughed.

"Oh, right. Nikki, breakfast? Clock's ticking."

"Of course, dear." Nikki ushered them to a corner booth shaped like a supposedly cosy undersea grotto. "I'll have your waiter over three seconds ago."

"There's a relativity problem there, Nikki," said Vee as she slid into her seat.

"What?" Nikki's face went politely blank.

"Science joke. Never mind." Vee smiled sunnily. "Have to get back into practice."

"Of course. Good luck, Vee." Nikki squeezed her shoulder and breezed away.

Rosa was looking at her. "What?" asked Vee.

Rosa picked up her napkin and made a great show of smoothing it across her lap. "It just never ceases to amaze me how fast you drop into the artiste persona."

"Hey." Vee stabbed the table with one finger. "That persona has kept us both living very comfortably. I wouldn't complain."

"Never," said Rosa flatly. "Just commenting." She called up the menu from the tabletop display and began examining it.

The cafe was tony enough to have real humans as servers, but, fortunately, not so over-the-top as to put them in any form of swimwear. Rosa and Vee ordered coffee, white tea, rolls, and fruit cups from a young man in the ultratraditional server's black-and-white uniform.

When he left, Rosa jacked her briefcase into the table and unfolded the view screen.

"How're we doing today?" Vee asked. If Rosa heard her, she gave no sign. She just skimmed the display and shuffled the icons.

"Your money's good," Rosa said at last. "The family trusts are percolating along nicely, and I think we're going to be able to put Kitty through college without a problem."

"Same as yesterday."

"Same as yesterday," agreed Rosa. "Want to see the latest on the Discovery?"

Vee shrugged, trying to be casual about it. "Might as well see what I'm getting into." Inside, her stomach began to flutter and she wondered where breakfast was. Food might help settle her down, except all of a sudden she wasn't hungry.

Rosa lit the back of the screen so Vee could follow along and called up her favorite news service.

The lead stories all came under the heading of *The Discovery on Venus,* as they had for the past month. Today was a pretty light news day. Only three new stories had been added since Vee checked it last night. Rosa touched the title *Venus Colonists Say No Help Needed* and the *Silent* option. The main menu vanished, and the text and video story unfolded in front of them.

Sources at Venera Base, home to the incredible discovery of what may be signs of alien life on Venus [long-range, color-enhanced picture of the spherical settlement with its airfoil tail floating through billowing clouds], are saying that the governing board strongly resents the formation of the new United Nations subcommittee on Venus. The governing board insists that the Venerans already in residence have sufficient expertise to deal with this most unexpected find.

While Dr. Helen Failia, founder of the base and head of Venera's Board of Directors [video clip of a short, gray-haired woman with a severe face giving a lecture to a group of what looked like college students], still refuses comment, sources close to the board say that petitions have been filed to render the Discovery [dissolve to the now familiar glowing hatchway] proprietary to the funding universities and therefore outside the realm of government probes or restrictions.

Dr. Bennet Godwin [jump cut to a split picture with a still shot of an iron-gray-haired man with permanent windburn in one half, and a hardsuited figure standing on a yellowish-red cliff in the other half], also on Venera's board, had this comment [the man's picture flickered to life].

"We welcome all serious research into any aspect of the world of Venus. That's what Venera Base is here for. What we cannot welcome, or tolerate, is interference by nonscientists in what is a *scientific* inquiry [the face froze]."

Dr. Godwin later issued the following clarification of his statement [the face flickered to life again, but now much more rigid and controlled]. "When I said nonscientists, obviously I meant unauthorized or inexpert personnel. This discovery is of massive importance to all humanity, and its investigation must be conducted in the open with all available assistance and resources."

"Who got you to add that disclaimer?" murmured Rosa, picking up her newly arrived cup of coffee and sipping it appreciatively. Vee swallowed some of the peach-flavored tea and poked at a strawberry in her fruit cup. The scent of fresh fruit and baked goods was failing to bring back her appetite in a rather spectacular fashion.

She read on.

When asked what he thought about Dr. Godwin's comment, Edmund Waicek [dissolve to the same man who had sent Vee her interview invitation], spokesman for the newly formed U.N. Work Group on Venus, said only, "We are glad that Dr. Godwin and the rest of the members of Venera Base realize how important openness and cooperation are at this historic time. This discovery affects the whole of humanity. Humanity's elected representatives need to assist in its uncovering and understanding."

"Mmmph." Rosa buttered a croissant and bit into it. Vee drank a little more tea, trying to get her stomach to open up enough that she'd actually be able to get some food down. The only thing that little piece made clear was that there was animosity between Venera Base and the U.N. That did not bode well, and Venera was probably going to live to regret it. It also meant she was walking into a hornets' nest, which made it even less likely that a controversial candidate would get the job.

"Eat, Vee," ordered Rosa. "You're not doing either of us any favors if you go in there on edge."

Vee obediently munched on strawberries, kiwis, mango, and pineapple. But she couldn't make herself face the rolls. Instead, she watched Rosa's screen. The other two stories were public-reaction sensation videos. One showed a public meeting in good old free-speech Chicago. The other was an interview with a pair of bald, neutered, Universal Age synthesists explaining how this was the first step toward the human worlds being accepted into the Greater Galactic Consciousness. There were, of course, links to the thousands of papers, discussions, and wonder-sites that had mushroomed since the Discovery was announced.

There had been aliens on Venus, and Earth was alive with all the wonder that the idea brought. At first, a lot of people had been worried that there would be riots and panics, but, so far, no one had seen fit to go twentieth over the news.

Something on Rosa chimed. "Time to go," she said, shutting down her briefcase. She picked up a danish and put it into Vee's hand. "Eat."

Vee gnawed the pastry without tasting it while Rosa authorized an account deduction on the table's screen. As they left, the fishes on the wall called, "Good luck, Vee," causing the other patrons to whisper and stare.

Vee made a mental note to tell Nikki never to do that again without permission and followed Rosa out the door.

Their appointment was in the J. K. McManus administration complex, which lay deep in the heart of U.N. City. It took Vee and Rosa twenty minutes, four glide-walks, and three ID scans before they reached the central atrium of the gleaming crystal-and-steel administration mall. Philodendrons, morning glories, and passion flowers twined around glass-encased fiber-optic bundles that stretched from floor to ceiling. Diplomats, administrators, lobbyists, and small herds of courier drones flowed in and out of transparent doors. They jammed the elevators and escalators running between the complex's eight floors. The muted roar of their voices substituted for the rush of wind and waves on the deck.

Vee and Rosa presented themselves to a live human security team and were asked to write down their names and leave a thumbprint on an impression film registry. In return, they were presented with audio badges and directed to Room 3425. The badges would tell them if they took a wrong turn.

Rosa clipped the badge to her briefcase strap and stepped onto the nearest escalator. Vee followed obediently, brushing restlessly at her tunic and smoothing down her veil.

They want me here. They want me here. I've done good, solid work and it's on record. I can do this. They believe I can do this, or they wouldn't have invited me in.

Room 3425 was a conference room. Rosa presented her badge to the room door, which scanned it, and her, before sliding open. On the other side waited an oval table big enough for a dozen people. An e-window showed a view of a tropical park on the sun-drenched deck with parti-colored parrots preening themselves in lush green trees.

The room had three occupants. Edmund Waicek sat at the conference table looking like he'd just stepped out of the story clip Vee viewed at breakfast. Next to him sat a tiny Asian woman in a pale-gold suit-dress. Her face was heavily lined, and her opaque red veil lay over pure-white hair. Behind them stood a slender, dark man who could have been from any of a hundred cities in the Middle East or North Africa. He wore a loose, white robe and a long orange-and-red-striped vest. A plain black cap covered his neatly trimmed hair. He turned from his contemplation of the parrots as the door opened and gave Vee a look that managed to be both amused and critical.

Mr. Waicek was on his feet and crossing the room toward Vee before Vee had a chance to step over the threshold.

"Dr. Hatch, thank you for coming." He shook Vee's hand with a nicely judged amount of firmness. "I'm Edmund Waicek."

"Pleased to meet you, Mr. Waicek," said Vee, extricating her hand.

"Call me Edmund," he said, as Vee guessed he would.

"Edmund," she repeated. "This is Rosa Cristobal."

"Delighted to meet you, Ms. Cristobal. Allow me to introduce you both to Ms. Yan Su. She is the Venus work group's resource coordinator."

"Pleased to meet you both." Ms. Yan's voice was light and slightly hesitant, giving the impression that English was not her first language. Underneath that, though, lay a feeling of strength and the awareness of it. "You will forgive me if I ask your field of specialty, Ms. Cristobal. The nature of your relationship with Dr. Hatch is not exactly clear."

Rosa gave a brief laugh. "No, it is not, even to me, some days. Primarily, I am Dr. Hatch's manager. I coordinate her projects and her contracts. Demand for her skills is very high, as I'm sure you know, but you would be amazed at the number of people who try to pay less than those skills are worth."

"And this is Mr. Sadiq Hourani, whose province is security," interjected Edmund smoothly.

Weird way of putting it. Mr. Hourani gave them a small bow. Vee noticed that his eyebrows were still raised and his expression was still amused.

Rosa laid her briefcase on the conference table and sat next to Ms. Yan. "First of all, let me say that we are extremely excited to be considered for this project." She jacked her case into the table, which lit up the clear-blue data displays in front of each of the participants.

"As we are to have you here," beamed Edmund. "We have reviewed Dr. Hatch's credentials in both the engineering and information fields and found them very impressive. Very impressive indeed."

"Thank you." Vee inclined her head modestly.

Edmund's smile grew fatherly. Vee kept her face still. "Our questions here will be of a more personal nature," he went on.

"What? Rosa didn't get you my gene screens?" Vee's flippancy was reflexive, and she regretted it even before Rosa's toe prodded her shin.

Ms. Yan laughed dryly. "No. Health issues, if there are any, will be addressed later. These are more questions of political outlook, approach, and general attitude toward—"

"Political outlook?" interrupted Vee.

"Yes," said Ms. Yan. "I wish this mission were purely a question of research and exploration, but it is not."

A spark of suspicion lit up inside Vee. She tried to squash it but was only partially successful. She'd grown up in the remnants of the old United States. Her grandfather had talked almost daily about the Disarmament, when U.N. troops went house to house confiscating guns and arresting the owners who would not peacefully hand them over, and worse. Personally, Vee thought her grandfather was nuts for romanticizing the freedom to shoot your neighbors, but his distrust and distaste for the "yewners" had taken root in some deep places, and she hadn't managed to shake it yet.

"Of course," Rosa was saying smoothly. "An effective team is more than just a collection of skills. Personalities have to mesh smoothly, and there must be a unified outlook."

"Exactly." Edmund's chest swelled, and Vee knew they were in for a speech.

Apparently, Ms. Yan knew it too because she quickly asked, "Have you ever been to Venera before, Dr. Hatch?"

"Once, about eight years ago." Vee did not miss the dirty look Edmund shot Ms. Yan, but she suppressed her smile of amusement. "As part of my Planets project." Vee's initial fame and the basis of her fortune was made by her creation of the first experiential holoscenic. It was a tour of the solar system, set to the music of Holst's *The Planets*. She had taken people inside the clouds of Venus, the oceans of liquid ice on Europa, the storms of Jupiter, and the revolt in Bradbury, Mars, for the movement "Mars, Bringer of War."

It suddenly hit Vee what they must be leading up to.

"I have always particularly liked the Veneran segment of *The Planets*," said Ms. Yan. "Most people see Venus as hellish. You made it beautiful."

"Thank you." Tension tightened Vee's back. *When are they going to say it? When are they going to say it?*

"Your section on the Bradbury Rebellion was rather less beautiful," said Edmund.

Vee caught Rosa's "be careful" glance and ignored it. "I strove for accuracy," she said, aware her voice had gone tart. "And comprehension." The "Bringer of War" segment showed the people being marched into the patched-up ships which were launched without regard to their safety, but it also showed the crowds rallying around Theodore Fuller and his cause, the shining faces, the great hopes of the dream of freedom before that dream had tarnished and twisted.

Edmund's expression fell into a kind of hard neutrality. "Yes, some of your images were quite . . . sympathetic." He glanced at a secondary display on the table in front of him. Vee wished she were close enough to read the items listed there. "What are your feelings about the separatist movements here on Earth?"

This is it? Vee looked incredulously from one face to the other. Both Edmund and Ms. Yan were perfectly serious. Even Mr. Hourani, who had not uttered one word since the beginning of the meeting, had lost his little amused smile. *They want to judge my fitness based on how I feel about separatists?*

Rosa's warning prod against her ankle grew urgent. Vee dismissed it and heaved herself to her feet.

"You want to know how I feel about Bradbury? I was seven

years old when that mess happened. I didn't have an opinion, just a few vague feelings. *The Planets* show was for money and to show off what you could do with my new holography tricks." She planted both hands on the table and leaned toward the yewners. "You want a political yes-sir, pick one of your own. You want an Earth Über Alles, find a Bradbury survivor. You want somebody who can take a look at your Discovery and just maybe come up with something useful to say about it, then you want me. But I will not"—she slammed her hand against the table—"sit here and be interrogated because I may have had a thought or two."

She turned on her heel and stalked out of the room.

The corridors passed by in a blur. She slapped her audio badge down on the counter at the security station without breaking stride. She saw nothing clearly until she found herself up on the deck in the blazing sunlight, staring out across the blue-gray waters and clenching her hands around the warm metal railing.

Well, Vee, you crashed that one pretty good, didn't you? She bowed her head until it rested on the backs of her hands. *What the hell were you doing? Did you really think they were looking for the dilettante?*

Vee was not going to whine about her fate. She had made her choices for money, yes, but also for love. She was good at her art. She understood light and the machines that manipulated it. She could shape light like a potter shaping clay. She knew how to blend it and soften it to create any color and nuance the human eye could detect. She knew how it controlled shadows and reflections. She knew how it scattered and bounced and played mischievous tricks on the senses. She knew nine-and-ninety ways it could be used to transmit messages. The lab had become mind-bogglingly boring right about the time the money from her patents and the resulting holo-scenics had really started to come in. She'd taken off for the artistic life, along with the ability to buy her college debts away from her parents' bank and keep her brothers and sisters from ever having to go into debt for themselves.

But sometimes she felt she'd missed the chance to do something real, the chance to explore as well as create, to question the nature of the universe in ways art couldn't reach by itself, to say something that would last, even if it was so obscure only ten other people understood it.

An accomplishment her family back in its naturalist, statist town wouldn't have to feel ambivalent about.

"You know," said Rosa's voice beside her, "there's this old saying that goes 'Be careful what you pretend to be; you may become it.'"

Vee lifted her head, blinking back tears of pain as the light assaulted her eyes. "How fast did they throw you out of there?"

"They didn't, actually." Rosa leaned her elbows against the railing. The salt breeze caught her silver scarf and sent it fluttering across her face. She pushed it away. "I spread some fertilizer about sensitive geniuses, which they seemed willing to sit still for. They, or at least Ms. Yan and Mr. Hourani, seemed impressed by your strong political neutrality." The wind plastered her scarf against her cheek again, and she brushed it back impatiently. "I'm less sure about Mr. Waicek, but I do believe he's leaning in our direction."

Hope, slow and warm, filled Vee's mind. "You're kidding."

"I have one question." Rosa rubbed her hands together and studied them. "Do you really want to do this?" She lifted her gaze to Vee's face. "They were giving you purity in there. This is going to be a political situation. You've seen the news. Everybody's got a position. Everybody wants referendums. You're going to be quizzed and dissected and watched, and you're going to have to put up with it. Quietly. No more scenes like that one." She jerked her chin back toward the glide-walk mouth.

"So, I'm asking you, Vee, as your friend and your manager, do you really, honestly, want to be a part of this mission?"

Vee stared out across the blue water under the brilliant sky. Nothing on Venus was blue. It was all orange and gold and blazing red. Yet someone had been there, had set up their base there, and then left. Where had they gone? Who were they? Why had they come in the first place? They might have left the answer behind them. It might be in that laserlike device.

Do I really want to be a part of finding that answer?

"Yes," she said, to sea and sky, and Rosa. "Oh yes. I want this."

Out of the corner of her eye, she saw Rosa nod. "Okay, then. I think you'll get it."

Vee's smile spread across her face. "If I do nothing else real in my life, at least I'll get to do this," she said softly.

For a moment, she thought she heard Rosa mutter, "Whatever *this* is," but then she decided that she didn't.

The image of a spring meadow high in the Colorado Rockies surrounded Yan Su as she sat behind her desk. She paid no attention to it. Instead, she focused on the wall screen, which she had set to record her message to Helen Failia on Venera Base.

"Hello, Helen. I just saw the latest commentary from out your way. Now, you know I don't interfere." Pause for Helen to insert whatever comment she had on that score. "But you've got to sit on Ben Godwin for the duration. I've done my best with the investigative team makeup. They are as close to what you asked for as I could manage. But this will not, I repeat, will not, hold up to certain types of scrutiny. Assure Dr. Godwin that if he lets the spinners do their job and is patient, this will all blow over and your people can get back to work.

"I'm doing my part down here, and we're making progress. You will all get what you want, but you've got to keep quiet." She paused again, tapping her fingernails against the glass of iced tea sitting on her desk. "I know this isn't easy, Helen, but believe me, it's the only way. You also need to keep your security chief on the alert. Every single cracker on three planets is going to be trying to get into Venera's systems, trying to get 'the real story.'" She made quotation marks with her fingertips. "The rumors in-stream are bad enough without that." She sighed softly. "Take care of yourself Helen. You've inherited quite a situation."

A quick keystroke faded the recording out and shunted the message into the queue for the next com burst out to Venus. Helen would receive the message in an hour or two.

Su finished her iced tea and rattled the ice cubes a couple of times as she stared at the sunlight on the distant snowy peaks. God, how long until she'd see the real thing again? She felt certain there would be nothing in her life but Venera and its Discovery at least until the "investigative team" came home, and maybe not even then. A lot would depend on how well Helen was able to handle her people and her sudden fame.

Su remembered the first time Helen Failia sailed into her office. Forty years ago, no, forty-five years ago, and she still remembered.

It had been a long day of in-stream meetings and screen-work. A headache was just beginning to press against her temples. None of this had left Su in the best of moods.

"Thank you for agreeing to see me, Ms. Yan." Helen Failia was not yet forty then. She wore her chestnut hair bundled up under a scarf of dusky-rose silk. Her handshake was firm, her smile genuine, and her movements calm and confident. Despite that, Su got the strong impression of restless energy brimming just below the surface of this woman.

"Now, what can I do for you, Dr. Failia?" Su asked as she handed Helen the cup of black coffee she'd requested. The woman was a very traditional American on that score.

"I'm building a research colony on Venus," said Helen, taking the seat Su waved her toward. "I want to know what governmental permissions I need."

Just like that. Not "I'm exploring the possibilities of . . ." or "I'm part of a consortium considering building . . ."

"You're building on Venus?" Su raised both eyebrows. "With what?"

She hadn't been able to get another word out for thirty minutes. Helen had brought scroll after scroll of blueprints, encyclopedic budget projections, and lists of potential donors. Everything was planned out, down to which construction facilities could supply which frame sections for the huge, floating city she had designed.

When Dr. Failia finally subsided, Su was ready to admit, privately, she was impressed. In an ideal world, Dr. Failia's proposal would be quite feasible. Unfortunately, Su had already been on the C.A.C. long enough to know this was not an ideal world.

Perhaps a gentle hint in that direction. "Wouldn't it be more practical, Dr. Failia, to start with a temporary facility funded by perhaps one or two universities?"

"No," said Helen at once. Su raised her eyebrows again, and Helen actually looked abashed. "I'm sorry, but no. Venus is a vast, complex world. It's active in many of the basic ways that Earth is active. It has an atmosphere, weather, and volcanic activity." Dr. Failia's eyes shone. At that, Su remembered where she'd heard Dr. Failia's name before. Helen Failia had been a member of the Icarus Expedition that had gone out, what was it? Two? No, three years ago. She was now one of the four people who had actually walked on the Venusian surface.

It also looked as though she had fallen in love down there.

"In a temporary facility," Dr. Failia was saying, "a few researchers could study a few aspects of the planet for a few months at a time. But in a real facility, such as Venera"—she tapped the screen roll—"people could specialize. Careers could be dedicated to the study of Earth's sister without requiring people to remove themselves from their families. The work could be made practical and comfortable for years at a time. We would not be limited to snapshots; we could take in the entire panorama."

Earth's sister. It is love. Su shook her head. "And the industrial applications? Are there any commercial possibilities?"

Helen didn't even blink. "In all probability, industrial and commercial applications would be limited. Mining or other exploitive surface operations would remain prohibitively expensive due to the harsh conditions."

All right, at least you're willing to admit that much, Dr. Failia. Su folded her hands on the desk and mustered her "serious diplomat" tones. "You do realize that the colonies which have paid off their debts and become going concerns all have some kind of export or manufacturing base?"

"Until now, yes."

Su found herself having to suppress a laugh. The question hadn't even ruffled the surface of Dr. Failia's confidence. "So you are hoping the research value will offset the economic liabilities?"

"Research and publicity." Helen thumbed through the screen rolls on the desk, pulled out the one labeled "University Funding" and presented it for Su's inspection. "Research departments in both universities and private industry are fueled by their papers as well as their patents. From a publications standpoint, Venus is more than ready to be exploited."

Su nodded as she skimmed the numbers again. It was all true and reasonable, as far as it went. But the fact was that the pure-research colonies had never worked. The small republics, and even the big universities, were unable to keep them funded. The United Nations was unwilling. Nobody said it out loud, of course, but the established wisdom was that the planets should be saved for industry, and now for the long-life retreats that the lobbyists were proposing as a way for those who had children but wanted extended life spans to have it all. They could live in specialized colonies with continued gene-level medical treatment without straining the balance and resources of Mother Earth.

Su found herself extremely ambivalent about that idea. But this one . . . Su liked the vision of this gigantic bubble of a town, sort of a U.N. City in the Venusian sky. She liked Helen's enthusiastic and detailed descriptions of not an outpost but a real community, as self-supporting as any off-world colony could be, given over to exploration and research. True, this vision ignored most of the political realities and historical examples, but that did not lessen its attractiveness. Su did not get much chance to dream anymore, and she found herself enjoying the opportunity.

Still, no politician could afford to dream for too long. *It'll be shot down by the rest of the C.A.C. if it gets in their line of sight,* she reminded herself with a sigh. They did not like approving doomed projects. It made for snide comments instream and low scores on the opinion polls.

But maybe, maybe there was a way around that.

"I will be honest with you, Dr. Failia," said Su. "Without the money in account, this is not going through."

To her credit, Helen Failia did not say "But . . ."

Su leaned forward, making sure the other woman met her gaze. "However, if you can get at least some of the start-up money, I think its chances are very good. Very good."

As Su watched, light sparked behind Dr. Failia's dark eyes. "Well, thank you for your time, Ms. Yan." She stood up and held her hand out. "I'll see you when I have my money."

Su also rose. "I look forward to it."

They shook hands. Helen gathered up her screen rolls and left without a backward glance. Su sat back down behind her desk and watched the door swish shut. Her headache, she noticed, had vanished.

"Desk. Sort recording of completed meeting and extract proposal details for the construction of Venera Base," she said thoughtfully. "Assume acquisition of adequate funding. List applicable regulatory and legislative requirements that must be met for construction of the proposed base." She paused. "Also extract voting records of C.A.C. members and project probable votes should proposal come to committee as offered in this meeting."

Helen, after all, was not the only one who had work to do if Venera was to . . . well . . . fly.

It had taken five years, but the money had been found; the base had been built, and for forty years after that, Helen kept it running. She scraped, scrounged, begged, borrowed, and worked the stream with a skill Su had seen only in the very best politicians. She had help of course. Sometimes, Su felt that while Helen had raised Venera, Su herself had raised Helen. She'd taught the older woman the finer points of publicity and spin doctoring. She'd steered her toward the more sympathetic funds and trusts. After the Bradbury Rebellion, Su had helped Helen make sure that all their money came from Earth so there could be no tangible connection between Venera and any suspect persons, who, at that point, included everyone who did not live on Mother Earth.

Helen had never married, never had children. Venera and its prosperity had been her entire life.

And she had almost lost it. Su tried to imagine what that felt like and failed. Her own life had been tied to so many different things—her husband, her son, political ambitions, and the colonies. Not just Venera, but Small Step and Giant Leap, Bradbury, Burroughs, Dawn, the L5 archipelagoes, all of them. They deserved their chance to flourish. Mother Earth needed her children, but like any flesh-and-blood parent, she needed to treat them as people, not possessions.

However, since Bradbury, with its deaths and exiles and threats, and since the long-life colonies had become a credit-filled reality, it had not been easy to convince anybody else in power of this.

For the moment, Venera at least was going to be all right. Su studied the donations list displayed on her desktop. If even half these promises were fulfilled, Venera was not going to even have to think about money for another five years.

Which is all to the good, Su rubbed her temples. *There is nothing bad about this. If we want any colony in the public eye, it's Venera.*

She shook herself. This was not anything she had time for. The Secretaries-General had called a meeting for the afternoon, and Su had to get her candidate files in order. Despite what she'd told Helen, there was still the very real possibility that Edmund might withdraw his backing from one or two of her people, and she might have to make her case to the Sec-Gens without any help at all. Secretary Haight was very much committed to the status quo, but Kent and Sun had a little more leeway in their thinking and saw the political opportunities inherent in loosening the grip on the planets a little. She would have to play to them if she wanted to keep the U.N. from just walking in and taking over the Discovery, and she wanted that very much.

The door chimed and Su looked at the view port. It cleared to reveal Sadiq Hourani and Su ordered it open. He walked in and Su waved him to a chair. Sadiq was on the very short list of people whom she would always see.

Su sat back and regarded him for a moment. "Tell me you have good news."

"I have good news," said Sadiq promptly.

"Really? Or are you just saying that?" Sadiq had been assigned to the C.A.C. security and intelligence work group ten years ago. In that time, Su had learned to trust him, despite the fact that he kept more hidden than she would ever learn about. It had not been easy, but it had been worth it.

Sadiq returned a small smile. "Really. We've negotiated an end to that potential media standoff in Bombay. They're to have some unmonitored access time to the investigative team and some of the Veneran scientists so they can ask questions without, and I quote, governmental interference, end quote."

Su raised both her eyebrows. "And you capitulated with all humbleness?"

"That I did."

"And you went in there knowing what they really wanted?"

"That I did," repeated Sadiq. "It's my job, you know."

The news of the Discovery had been received with calm just about everywhere. There were a few hardcase places—Bombay, Dublin, Old L.A.—where tempests threatened to start up in the stream. The stream was the systemwide communications network that had evolved out of all the old nets and webs that had spanned the globe since the twentieth century. It was possible for discontent in-stream to spill out into the real world. Part of Sadiq's job was to make sure it never did.

"So." Su leaned back and folded her hands in her lap. "Do you know what the Secretaries-General really want to see us about?"

Sadiq shrugged. "To hear about Bombay, for a start, and the other hot spots. They should have reviewed our Comprehensive Coping Strategy by now. They also, of course, need to give their blessing to the investigative team roster so the full committee won't be able to bicker too much."

"Have you ascertained whether Edmund's going to behave?" Su had known from the beginning that Edmund was going to be difficult. Since he had been appointed to the C.A.C., he had been one of the loudest anticolonial voices they had, and that was saying a great deal. His initial idea had been to send out a team that would investigate Venera at least as thoroughly as it would investigate the Discovery.

"I believe he will." Sadiq studied his neat hands for a moment. "You know, Su, you are going to have to speak to him again, sooner or later."

"Yes, I know." After Dr. Hatch and Ms. Cristobal had left, Edmund had started in on one of his canned speeches about the "absolute necessity of choosing members who will not be blinded by propaganda or sentimentality and will be willing to examine *every* aspect of the Discovery." Su, suddenly unable to stand it another minute, had stood up and said, "You don't want an investigation; you want an inquisition," and stalked out.

The memory made her sigh again. "That is no way for a grown bureaucrat to behave. Especially now," she added.

"Especially now," echoed Sadiq. "Especially on one of your pet projects."

Su eyed him carefully to see if there was anything hidden under that statement, but Sadiq's face remained placid. "Yes," she admitted. "This one's mine and I can't hide from it." She was about to add a question about Edmund Waicek, positive that Sadiq had spoken with him before he walked into her office, but Sadiq had stiffened and his eyes darted back and forth. Su closed her mouth. Sadiq wore a phone spot, so he could be reached at any time. This could be anything from a request for authorization on an expense report to notification of an outbreak of public violence.

When Sadiq had focused on her again, Su asked, "Anything wrong?"

"We seem to have a demonstration on the deck." Sadiq stood. "Peaceful but illegal. Care to come?"

"Not really." Su waved him away. "I'll see you at the Sec-Gens this afternoon."

"Until then." Sadiq left her there. The door swished shut

behind him. Su sat still for a moment, then swiveled her chair toward her working wall. "Window function," she ordered, "show me political activity identified on main deck."

A patch of Colorado sky cleared away, replaced by the image of one of the observation towers. Normally, the side of the three story building was a blank, forbidding gun-metal gray. Today, however, someone had managed to hang a gigantic sheet screen from the side and light up a scene of Venus and Earth orbiting around each other in a display that was as pretty as it was inaccurate. A crowd had gathered at the foot of the tower to watch the show. In front of the casual observers, a set of feeders with briefcases and camera bands had already jacked into the deck and were rapidly dropping the entire experience into the stream.

Venus and Earth faded, replaced by a man of moderate coloring and moderate age, wearing a suit so conservative he might have bought it in the previous century.

"And what are we doing with this wonder, this Discovery?" He swept one hand out. Venus appeared, neatly balanced in his palm. "We are using it as a focus of fear. We are using it to tighten the chains already on the wrists of our brothers and sisters in the colonies. Millions of people whose only crime is not living on Mother Earth." He closed his fist around the Venus globe. The low moan it gave was gratuitous, Su thought, but it did make its point. "We must, every one of us, ask what is our government so afraid of? Aging men and women who failed in their dream?" The starry background blurred and shifted until the speaker stood in a bare red-ceramic cell filled with people whose eyes were dark and haunted. "The guilty have been punished and punished again. Must we punish their children now?"

Before the speaker could answer his own question, the screen went black. A groan rose from the assembled crowd. Three people in coveralls of U.N. blue appeared on the observation tower's roof and started rolling up the screen. Still grumbling, the crowd began to disperse. Show's over.

"Window function off."

The screen melted back into the meadow scene around her.

Su considered. That wasn't much as demonstrations went, but it would give her an opening to talk with Edmund. Su rubbed her forehead. Her mind had been shying away from the memory of how she'd left the morning's interview. What had happened? What had snapped? There was no excuse, none, especially now, as she'd said to Sadiq. If she didn't find a way to clean up after herself, it would be . . . bad.

"Desk. Contact Edmund Waicek." *Compose yourself, Su. Don't let the boy get to you. There is too much going on for that.* "Put display on main screen."

The whole wall cleared until Su saw Edmund's clean, blank-walled office. Edmund himself was hunched over his desk screen. He did not look up.

"I'm rather busy, Su. We do have a meeting this afternoon."

"Yes, I am aware of that." *Calm, calm, calm.* "Were you aware that we've just had a separatist demonstration on the main deck?"

Edmund's head jerked up. "What?"

Su waved her hands in a gesture both dismissing and soothing. "It was small. Sadiq's people have already handled it." She lowered her hands. "But it did draw a crowd. Here. People were listening. The speaker was making sense to them."

Edmund's face went cold. Su held up her hand again before he could even open his mouth. "It does matter. This is U.N. City, and our people were listening to the idea that perhaps the restrictions on the colonies have gone too far." She spread her hands. "There is more than one kind of bias we need to avoid here, Edmund. If it appears that we are sending up a team that has an anticolonial agenda, we run the risk that their conclusions will be discounted by popular opinion. We have both been around the world far too many times to pretend that doesn't matter."

She watched Edmund's expression waver as that thought sank in. "We cannot be seen to encourage irresponsible rhetoric," he said, resorting to some rhetoric of his own.

Good. He's running short on arguments. "Of course not. We must be seen to be aiming for a strict neutrality. That is where people like Veronica Hatch can benefit us. People appreciate that she put a human face on a terrible tragedy. On both sides of the tragedy."

Edmund did not like that idea. She could tell that much by the stony set of his jaw, but he was at least thinking about it. "If we're taking her and the other one"—he glanced at his desk—"Peachman, I want security on the team."

"My thinking exactly," lied Su. "Sadiq can pick the best available, and we can submit their names to the Sec-Gen along with the others."

"All right," said Edmund. "You've got your team, Su. But it had better not overstep its bounds."

"It won't, Edmund. I'll see you this afternoon."

Edmund nodded and broke the connection. Su collapsed back into her chair. *That was a near thing.* If Edmund had been just a little more angry, it would not have worked. But it did, and that was all she needed to care about at this moment.

Still, there was one more call she should make.

"Desk. Contact Yan Quai."

This time, the sky was replaced by a static scene of a white railed veranda overlooking a misty cityscape.

"I'm sorry," said a gender-neutral voice. "Yan Quai is unavailable—"

"Quai, it's your mother."

The voice hesitated. Then, the veranda cleared away and revealed Quai's apartment, which hadn't been cleaned up in a while. Clothes and towels were draped over the arms of chairs. Screen rolls lay heaped on every flat surface, held in place by empty cups and glasses full of something that might have once been either beer or apple juice.

In the middle of it all sat Quai at his battered desk. Su automatically looked him over. He hadn't shaved. His hair was now black and blond, and the holo-tat on the right side of his throat was a winking blue eye this week.

In short, her son looked just fine.

"Hello, Mother," he said cheerfully. "Slow day in the corridors of power?"

"Not particularly." Her lips twitched, trying not to smile. "As you've said, saving the worlds is a full-time job."

Quai's own smile was tight and knowing and made him look frighteningly like his father. "Especially when you have to kiss up to the C.A.C. to do it."

Su let that pass. "We've just had a little demo on the decks here, Quai."

"Really?" His face and voice brightened considerably. "Who managed it?"

"I don't know. I thought you might."

Quai shook his head, and Su believed him. If he had known, he would have just evaded the question. They did not agree, she and her son. He felt she did not go far enough in her politics, and she felt that by attempting to undermine the system, he was worsening the condition of those he was supposed to be fighting for. Despite that, they had a tacit agreement that each would avoid lying to the other, if at all possible.

"Well, just in case anyone in your acquaintance gets ideas—"

"Us?" Quai laid a hand on his breast. "We operate strictly within the law wherever we are, Mom; you know that."

"I don't for sure know any different," responded Su blandly. "But just in case, you might pass along the word that the C.A.C. is very edgy right now and that that edginess is getting communicated up the legislature. The more unrest there is right at this moment, the bigger the potential backlash."

They looked at each other, each of them replaying conversations from both the distant and the not-so-distant past in their heads.

"All right, Mom." Quai nodded. "Not that anybody I deal with would arrange illegal public demos in U.N. City or anywhere else, but I'll see if I can leak the generalities of this conversation where they'll do some good."

"That's all I ask." Su bowed her head briefly in a gesture of thanks.

A flicker of worry crossed Quai's face. "Take care of yourself out there, Mom. Okay? I'd hate to see you lose your footing."

Su smiled. "I will take care. I love you, my son."

"Love you, Mom. Good-bye."

Su said good-bye and shut down the screen. She shook her head and sighed. Quai was good people. How had that happened? Abandoned by a nervous father, left with an obsessive mother, he still managed to make his own way. He went overboard, it was true, but not as badly as some, and at least he really believed in what he did.

So do you, she reminded herself. *At least, you'd better, or all your work's going to fall apart and Helen's going to be left out there on her own.*

That thought stiffened Su's shoulders. No, she would not permit that. She bent over her desk screen and laid her hands on the command board. Time to get back to work.

CHAPTER FOUR

T'sha's kite furled its bright-blue wings as it approached the High Law Meet. Unlike other cities, the High Law Meet's ligaments ran all the way down to the crust, tethering the complex in place. The symbolism was plain. All the winds, all the world, met here.

"Good luck, Ambassador T'sha," the Law Meet hailed her through her headset. "You are much anticipated."

"Is it a pleased anticipation or otherwise?" asked T'sha wryly as the Law Meet took over her kite guidance, bringing it smoothly toward the empty mooring clamps.

"That is not for me to know or tell," said the Meet primly. Amusement swelled through T'sha.

T'sha had always found the Meet beautiful. Its shell walls were delicately curved, and their colors blended from a pure white to rich purple. Portraits and stories had been painted all across their surfaces in both hot and cold paints. When the Law Meet was in dayside, the hot paints glowed red. On nightside, the cold paints made dark etchings against the shining walls. The coral struts were whorled and carved so that the winds sang as they blew past. More shell and dyed stiff skins funneled and gentled the winds through the corridors between the chambers. The interior chambers themselves were bubbles of still air where anyone could move freely without being guided or prodded by the world outside.

T'sha sometimes wondered if this was a good idea.

As ever, the High Law Meet was alive with swarms of people. The air around it tasted heavy with life and constant movement. T'sha counted nine separate villages floating past the Meet with their sails furled so the citizens who flew beside their homes could keep up easily. All the noise, all the activity of daily life blew past with them.

Below, the canopy was being tended by the Meet's own conservators. It was symbolically important, said many senior ambassadors, that the canopy around the High Law Meet remain vital, solid, and productive. But as T'sha watched, a quartet of reapers from one of the villages, identifiable by the straining nets they carried between them, as well as by the zigzagging tattoos on their wings, descended to the canopy. A conservator flew at them, sending them all winging away, back to their village with empty nets, no food, seeds, or clippings to enhance their diet, their gardens, or their engineers' inventories.

T'sha felt her bones loosen with weariness. *It must be kept productive. Certainly. But if not for our families, then for what?*

T'sha inflated, trying to let her mood roll off her skin. There was important work to be done, and she had to be tightly focused. Her kite dropped its tethers toward the Law Meet's mooring clamps. T'sha leaned back on her posthands so she could collect her belongings: an offering for the temple, the congratulatory banner for Ambassador Pr'sef's latest wedding, and the bulging satchel of promissory agreements which she had negotiated in return for the votes she needed. She had promised away a great deal of work from her city and her families for this vote. She had to keep telling herself that they all gave freely and that she was doing this for the entirety of the people, not just for herself. This was necessary. It was not greed.

The clamps took hold of the tethers and reeled the kite in to a resting height. T'sha launched herself into the wind, her parcels dangling from three of her hands.

A temple surmounted the High Law Meet. It was a maze of ligaments and colored skins, covered in a complex blanket of life. In the corners and catches, puffs, birds, flies, algae bubbles, smoke growers, and a hundred other plants and animals collected. Funguses and danglers grew from the walls and fed the creatures who lived there, until the winds that blew them in blew them away again.

As she let those winds carry her toward the temple's center, T'sha tried to relax and immerse herself in the messages of life present in every plant, every insect and bird. She had only marginal success. There was too much waiting on the vote in the Meet below to allow her to give in to her meditations.

The temple's center was ablaze with tapestries, each illustrating a history, parable, or lesson. Congregants were supposed to let the random winds blow them toward a tapestry and consider its moral. This time, however, T'sha steered herself toward a small tapestry that fluttered alone in a deep curve of the wall. It was ancient, woven entirely from colored fibers taken from the canopy. It depicted a lone male, his hands bony, his skin sagging, and his muzzle open in muttered speech. His rose and violet crest draped flat against his back as if he lacked the strength to raise it. All around him stretched the crust, naked to the sky.

As T'sha drank in the tapestry's details, a teacher drifted to her side. "Tell me this story," he said.

The words spread the warmth of familiarity through T'sha. Her youth had seemed dominated by those words. Her birth mother, Pa'and, had brought T'sha teacher after teacher, each more taxing than the last. Whether the lesson was maths, sciences, history, or even the geographies of the wind currents, they all seemed to start their quizzing by saying "Tell me this story."

"Ca'doth was the first of the Teacher-Kings," began T'sha, keeping her attention fixed on the tapestry, as was proper. "Contemplate the object and its lesson. This is the way to learn." Which of the parade of teachers had first told her that? "He led twenty cities in the Equatorial Calms. But he wanted to harvest eight canopy islands that were also claimed by D'anai, who was Teacher-King for the Southern Roughs. A feud began. Each king made great promises to their neighbors to join their cause. Arguments and debates lasted years. Ca'doth, who was the greatest speaker ever known, persuaded the winds and the clouds and even the birds to help him." T'sha's imagination showed her Ca'doth, strong and healthy, spreading his wings to the listening clouds.

"What he wanted most was that the living highlands should stop feeding his enemies," she went on, falling into the rhythm of her recitation. The teacher hovered close beside her, encouraging her with his silence. "But no matter how long he flew around the highlands, they made no response to his great speeches." The smallest of the monocellulars originated in the living highlands, which expelled them into the air to be the seeds for all other life in the world.

"At last, he realized he would have to fly inside the highland to make it hear him. He dived straight down the throat of the living highland, beating his wings against winds of solid lava. He passed through a chamber where the walls were pale skin, a chamber of white bone, a chamber of silver plasma, and a chamber tangled with muscle and nerve. In each he heard a riddle to which he did not know the answer." For a moment, she thought the teacher would ask her the riddles, but he did not, and she kept going. "Finally, Ca'doth came to a chamber where the air around him shimmered golden with the pure essence of life, and he knew he floated within the soul of the living highland.

"'Why do you feed my enemies?' he cried. 'They steal what I need to live. I have promised away all my present that I may gain a future for my children, and yet you feed those who would destroy them. Why?'

"The soul of the highland answered him, 'Life cannot choose who it helps. If your enemy came to me first, should I starve you instead?'

"But Ca'doth did not listen. He argued and pleaded and threatened, until the highland said 'Very well, I will not feed your enemy.'

"Pleased, Ca'doth passed through the chambers, and there he heard the answers to all the riddles but could not tell which answer fitted which riddle. He emerged into the clear and returned to tell his family the highland would no longer feed their rivals.

"But when he reached his birth city, the city and all within were dead, starved.

"The highland would not feed the rivals, but the highland would no longer feed Ca'doth's people either. Ca'doth turned from his rule and his other cities and drifted on the winds for the rest of his life, trying to fit the answers to the riddles."

The teacher dipped his muzzle approvingly. "And what is the meaning of this story?"

"All life is linked," answered T'sha promptly. "If that is forgotten, all life will die." *Even the flies,* she sighed inwardly. *Even the fungus. Even I and D'seun.*

T'sha deflated before the teacher and flew respectfully underneath him. She slipped around the side of the temple to the gifting nets and deposited her offering—a pouch of seeds and epiphytes that her own family had recently spread in the canopy. They were having great success in healing a breech in the growth. Hopefully, the temple's conservators could make use of them as well.

As she sealed the gifting net up and turned, she found herself muzzle-to-muzzle with Z'eth, one of the most senior ambassadors to the Meet. T'sha pulled back reflexively, fanning her wings to get some distance.

"Good luck, Ambassador T'sha," said Z'eth, laughing a little at how startled her junior colleague was. Z'eth was big and round. Even when she had contracted herself, she was a presence that filled rooms and demanded attention. She had only three tattoos on her pale skin—her family's formal name, the rolling winds, indicating she was a student of life, and the ambassador's flock of birds on her muzzle. Despite her sparse personal decoration, there was something extravagant about Z'eth. Perhaps that was only because there was no promise so rare or exotic she would not make it if it benefited her city. T'sha could not blame her for that. The city K'est had sickened when T'sha was still a child, and Z'eth's whole existence had become dedicated to keeping her city alive.

"Good luck, Ambassador Z'eth," said T'sha. "I was on my way to your offices from here."

"No doubt to speak of things it is not appropriate to discuss in temple." Z'eth dipped her muzzle. "Shall we leave so we may converse freely?"

"Thank you, Ambassador."

Z'eth and T'sha let themselves be blown through the temple corridors and out into the open air.

As soon as they were a decent distance from the temple's walls, T'sha said, "I have the promissory for you regarding the imprinting service for the cortices grown in your facilities."

"Excellent." Z'eth tilted her wings and deflated so she descended smoothly alongside the High Law Meet. It was a delicate path, as the winds between the walls were strong and unpredictable. T'sha followed but had to flap clumsily to keep herself from being brushed against the painted-shell wall.

"I have not envied you these past hours, Ambassador." Z'eth whistled sympathetically. "It is hard during your first term, especially if your first term is a historic one." One of the arched corridor mouths opened behind them, but Z'eth wheeled around, dipping under the corridor instead of entering it. T'sha followed her into the shallow, irregular tunnel underneath the real corridor, a little surprised.

Z'eth drifted close, her wings spread wide. Her words brushed across T'sha's muzzle. "You needn't worry about the vote. Your quiet promises and the work Ca'aed has done with Gaith have been most impressive. I have spoken where I can. Between us all we have turned the flow. You'll have your appointment."

T'sha nearly deflated with relief. At the same time she was conscious of Z'eth's steady gaze on her. Despite the promises she had already made, she still owed the senior ambassador, and it was a debt that would need to be paid before long.

T'sha resolved not to worry about that now. "Thank you again, Ambassador Z'eth."

"You are welcome. I will see you in the voting chamber." Z'eth lifted herself to the corridor mouth and disappeared inside.

T'sha floated where she was for a moment, remaining in place more because she was in a calm than from actual effort.

They had towed Gaith's corpse encased in its quarantine blanket into Ca'aed's wake. The rotting had so deformed it that it looked less like a city than an engineer's experiment gone hideously wrong. Its people worked on it diligently, sampling and analyzing and salvaging, but it would have taken a thicker skin than T'sha's not to feel the despair in them. It had taken Gaith a handful of hours to die. Who knew which village, which city, might be next?

And here was T'sha, doing her best to keep them all from what looked like the nearest safe course. She had quizzed the team supervisors from the other candidate worlds extensively. The seeds had not taken hold on any other of the ten worlds. Only Number Seven could readily support life.

But life might already have a claim on Number Seven. In spite of all, T'sha could not let that fact blow past. She had to see for herself that D'seun's team was not ignoring a legitimate claim on the part of the New People. Now, according to Z'eth, she was going to get her chance.

Is this right, what I do? Life of my mother and life of my father, it has to be, because it is too late for me to do otherwise.

She shut her doubts off behind calculations about how many promises she could deliver before she was called to hear the vote. She lifted herself to the corridor mouth and joined the swarm of ambassadors and assistants propelling themselves deep into the Meet.

In the end, she was able to deliver four of the eight notes, staying long enough to give and accept polite thanks with each ambassador and discuss general pleasantries and the work being done on Gaith. She had to use her headset to leave message for the rest. The Law Meet was calling them all to hear the results of the latest poll.

When T'sha arrived, the spherical voting chamber already brimmed with her colleagues. There were no perches left. She would have to float in the stillness and try to keep from bumping rudely into anyone else.

"Good luck, T'sha," murmured tiny, tight Ambassador Br've as she drifted above him.

"Good luck," added Ambassador T'fron, whose bird tattoos were still fresh on his skin.

Their wishes warmed her, but not as much as the security of Z'eth's promise.

T'sha found a clear spot in which to hover near the ceiling.

Because the High Law Meet was currently on the dayside, the family trees, which were written in hot paints, glowed brightly against the white and purple walls. Each showed the connections and the promises of connection between the First Thousand. T'sha scanned the trees for her family's names and found them, unchanging and immutable. She was their daughter. Her ancestors had birthed cities. She would save them, but not at the cost of their people's souls.

She looked down between the crests and tattooed wings and spotted D'seun's distinctive and overmarked back. He was practically touching the polling box. T'sha wondered whom he had made promises to and if he had anyone as powerful as Z'eth sponsoring his cause. If he'd managed to bring in H'tair or Sh'vaid on his side, the vote might not be as set as Z'eth believed. The mood of the meeting tightened rapidly around her. The announcement would come soon. Her bones shifted. Soon. Soon.

The polling box had been grown in the image of a person without wings or eyes. Its neural net ran straight into the floor of the voting chamber and was watched over by the High Law Meet itself. It would not be moved, and it looked with favor on no one. It was solid and impartial.

The box lifted its muzzle and spoke in a voice that rippled strongly through the chamber.

"The poll has been taken, recognized, and counted. Does any ambassador wish to register doubt as to the validity of the count contained in this box?"

No one spoke. T'sha tried to breathe evenly and hold her bones still.

"No doubt has been registered," said the box. "A poll has been taken of the ambassadors to the High Law Meet on the following questions. First, should candidate world Seven be designated New Home? If this is decided positively, the second question is, should the current investigative team whose names are listed in the record continue under the leadership of Ambassador D'seun Te'eff Kan K'edch D'ai Gathad to establish the life base necessary for the growth of a canopy and the establishment of life ways for the People, with such expansion and promises as this project shall require?"

T'sha's wings rippled. Her skin felt alert, open to every sensation from the brush of her own crest to the gentle waft of a whisper on the other side of the chamber.

"Is there any ambassador within the touch of these words who has not been polled on these questions?" asked the box. Silence, waiting, and tension strained her bones as if they were mooring ligaments in a high wind.

"No ambassador indicates not having been polled," said the box. "Then, the consensus of the High Law Meet is as follows. On the first question, the consensus is yes, candidate world Seven is New Home."

The rumble and ripple of hundreds of voices filled the chamber. T'sha remained still and silent. That was never the real question. The vote had to be yes. D'seun was right about that much. His peremptory poll of Ca'aed had confirmed that all the families agreed with the choice.

"On the second question," the box went on, "the consensus is that Ambassador D'seun Te'eff Kan K'edch D'ai Gathad shall continue as the leader of the investigative team, that the current team will continue in the task of creating a life base with such expansions as are required for that task, provided that one of those expansions shall be the addition of Ambassador T'sha So Br'ei Taith Kan Ca'aed for the purpose of observing and studying the life currently named the New People. She shall ensure that these New People have no legitimate claim to New Home world that might counteract the validity of the consensus on the first question."

There it was. She could now go to New Home herself and make sure the New People had no legitimate claim on the world. T'sha's relief was so complete, she almost didn't feel the congratulations erupting around her. When she was able to focus outward, she found herself in a storm of good-luck wishes and a hundred questions. She answered all she could, as fast as she could, while mentally cataloging the messages and calls she'd have to make as soon as the chamber opened again.

It might have been a moment or a lifetime later when D'seun rose to meet her.

"An interesting addendum, Ambassador T'sha," he said flatly and coolly. "You have been working toward this for some time, I take it."

T'sha met D'seun's gaze and spoke her words straight to him. "Surely, you could not have been unaware of what I was doing. I was hardly secretive."

D'seun's bones contracted under his tattoos, and T'sha felt a swirl of exasperation. She shrank herself a little to match him. "D'seun, there is no reason for us to be enemies on this. We both want the same thing. We both want to make New Home a reality. If that is to happen, we cannot discount the New People."

"We cannot let their presence override everything we must do, either." He thrust his muzzle forward. "You question and delay, you counter and debate everything! Every time we try to warn people what happened to Gaith, there you are, assuring us all that it isn't so very bad, that we must just wait until its disease is understood, that we have the resources to understand." His words tumbled harshly over her. "There is no more time. There is no way to understand. We must leave."

T'sha deliberately deflated and sank, resisting the urge to fly right under him to make her point. "I am only one voice, D'seun. All the rest of the Senior Committee for New Home are your supporters. There will be very little I can do."

D'seun dropped himself so he could look into her eyes. "Do

not flutter helplessness at me, T'sha. What 'little' you can do, you will do."

"Is there some promise you would give my families to have me do otherwise, D'seun?" asked T'sha bluntly. "How much will you give for me to disregard our new neighbors? Is there enough to make that right?"

D'seun did not answer.

"No, there is not," said T'sha. "We are together in this, D'seun, until the task is over."

"Until the task is over," D'seun said softly. "Until then."

D'seun rose from the world portal into the candidate world, now New Home. Its clean winds brushed the transfer's disorientation off him. A quick turn about showed him P'tesk and T'oth waiting on the downwind side of the portal's ring. D'seun flew quickly toward them.

"Good luck, Ambassador D'seun." P'tesk raised his hands. "Is there news?"

D'seun touched his engineers' hands. "Engineer P'tesk, Engineer T'oth. There is news, but not all of it is good. Let us return to the test base, and then I can tell our people all at once."

As often as he had done it, it was strange to D'seun to fly over the naked crust without even a scrap of canopy to cover it. He could barely taste the life base they had seeded the winds with. He imagined sometimes that this was not a newly emerging world, but a prophecy as to what Home might become—lifeless stone and ash sculpted by sterile winds.

So it will be if T'sha has her way.

Their base was little more than a few shells tethered together with half a dozen infant cortex boxes to nurture the necessary functions. Not comfortable or companionable, but it served its function, as they all did.

"Team Seven," D'seun called through his headset, "this is

Ambassador D'seun. We are gathering in the analysis chamber. I have word of the latest vote from the High Law Meet."

Like the rest of the base, the analysis chamber was strictly functional. The undecorated walls showed the shell's natural pearl and purple colors. Separate caretaker units, all holding their specialized cortex boxes, had been grown into the shell. That and a few perches were all there was to the room.

D'seun, T'oth, and P'tesk arrived to find T'stad and Kr'ath already waiting for them. They all wished each other luck as the others filtered in. D'seun's gaze swept the assembly—his assembly, his team who had worked so hard to prove the worth of their world. He laid claim to them all, and if that was greedy of him, so be it. After so much work and so many promises, he had earned the right to be a little greedy.

"Where is Engineer Br'sei?" D'seun asked.

The others glanced around the chamber, as if just now noticing Br'sei was gone.

"Engineer Br'sei?" he asked his headset.

After a brief pause, Engineer Br'sei's voice came back. "I'm at Living Highland 45, Ambassador. I'll listen in over the headset. I have to check the stability of the base seeding here. I think we may be running into some trouble from the high salt content of these lavas."

"Then listen closely." D'seun raised his voice to speak to the entire assembly. "The ambassadors to the High Law Meet have voted. This world, our world, is declared New Home!"

All around him, voices trilled high, fluting notes of jubilation. D'seun let them enjoy. They had all worked so hard. Thousands of dodec-hours of observation and analysis. Millions of adjustments in proportion and organization on the most basic levels. Sometimes it felt as though each molecule had been hand reared. But they had made their promise to the whole of the People, and they had kept it. Life could be made to thrive here in these alien winds.

"That is not all the news, however," D'seun said, cutting through their celebration. He waited until the last echoes of their chaotic song died away. "Something new has happened on Home."

All their attention was on him, and he told them about Gaith. For the first time there was no danger of interference from T'sha, and he could tell what had really happened. An entire village had died an indescribable death in such pain as life should never know. It had happened in a few hours. A life the villagers thought they knew, a life they had grown and cherished for thousands of years, had gone insane. Insane as it was, it would turn on other life until nothing was left but a mantle of death surrounding the entire world.

When he was finished, not one of them remained their normal size. They all huddled close to their perches and close to each other, small and tight, as if they could draw their skin in far enough to shut his words out.

"I know the dangers of haste," he said at last. "I was taught, as you all were, that haste is equal to greed as a bringer of death. But this time, to be cautious is to die. This new rot will not wait for us to make our careful plans."

Soft whistles of agreement filled the room. D'seun let himself swell, just a tiny bit. "There are those who do not understand this, however. There are those among the ambassadors who insist that we wait. For what? I ask. Until our cities all fall? No, they reply. Until we are sure of the New People."

Silence. The New People. No one liked the mention of them. The New People might be poison, and everyone here felt that in every pore.

Time to remove that poison. "We are all concerned about the New People. We have watched them as closely as we are able. You have labored with great care to understand their transmissions to each other and their commands to their tools. You have spoken to me in a straightforward fashion, as dedicated engineers should, about the fragility of life and the resources of community and the claim of life upon its own home. But I must ask you other questions now."

D'seun focused his attention completely on P'tesk. "P'tesk, have we found any new life here? Any life we did not ourselves spread?"

"No, Ambassador," said P'tesk. "Except for our life base, the winds are clean. The living highlands do not really measure up to that name—none of the ones we've observed anyway."

"T'vosh." D'seun switched his focus to the youngest engineer. "Have we seen signs of mining or sifting for the hard elements?"

"No, Ambassador," T'vosh answered quickly. "And among the transmissions, we have heard no plans for such."

"No plans that we understand."

The last was spoken by Tr'es. D'seun did not let himself swell in frustration. It was a good point. Besides, Tr'es's birth city was Ca'aed, as was T'sha's. She would have to be handled carefully in the time to come.

"None that we understand, yes." D'seun dipped his muzzle. "Our understanding is far from perfect. Our ability to separate image and message and tool command is not complete, although we have made great strides. The New People may be making plans for legitimate use of this world." His gaze swept the assembly. "But they have not done it yet. When has a mere plan, an unfulfilled intent, ever been grounds to withhold a resource?" He let them think about that for a minute. "Most importantly"—he spread his wings wide—"nothing has prevented them from detecting the life base. Nothing has prevented them from finding us. They have made no move to challenge our claims or to contact us as one family contacts another when there is a dispute over resources." *Let those words sink through their pores; let their minds turn that over.*

"There is nothing, nothing, in the laws of life and balance which prevents us from moving forward and laying legitimate claim to this empty, pure world."

Whistles of agreement, notes of encouragement bathed D'seun. This would work. He had them convinced. "Despite this, for reasons of her own, the ambassador of Ca'aed"—he glanced at Tr'es—"is doing all she can to delay the transformation of this world, and she is citing the presence of the New People as her reason."

Tr'es was not intimidated, not yet. "How could she do otherwise?" Tr'es asked. "They are here. Ambassador T'sha is both cautious and pious."

"Ambassador T'sha has acquired the body of Gaith Village for the people of Ca'aed," replied D'seun. "She has indentured all Gaith's engineers to the resurrection of the village. She hopes to exact many promises for herself and her city, even while the new rot spreads on the winds."

Silence, deep and shocked, filled the chamber, broken only by the slight rustling as the engineers inflated and deflated uneasily.

"Surely there is a misunderstanding," stammered Tr'es. "This cannot be the stated goal."

"It is not the stated goal," said D'seun softly. "But I fear it is the true goal. I grieve with you and your city, Engineer Tr'es, but power has turned many a soul sour. This is why the teachers warn us so stringently against greed. Through greed we turn the very needs of life against each other."

Tr'es covered her eyes with her wing in confusion and denial. D'seun said nothing, just let the silence settle in ever more deeply. At last, Tr'es lifted her muzzle. "What are we to do?"

D'seun felt satisfaction form deep in his bones. "Ambassador T'sha is coming here herself to inspect the claims of the New People. We must make sure she is given no reason to doubt that this world is free for us to use." He focused his attention on each of his engineers in turn. "She must have no opportunity to question what we do here." He pulled his muzzle back and drew in his wings. "I will make no move without your agreement. You are not indentured, and I do not lead without consensus. We will take a poll now. Vote as your soul's understanding moves you. Let me hear from those in agreement."

One by one, his engineers whistled their assent. Even Tr'es whistled agreement, low but strong.

"I thank you," said D'seun softly. "Soon, all your families will have cause to thank you as well. We can move forward with our work now, without doubt or hindrance. Enjoy, my friends. Soon promises will be made in your names and on the backs of your skills."

More wordless songs of delight and triumph rang out. D'seun swelled to his fullest extent to take in every note and nuance. It was then he realized that his headset had remained silent. Br'sei had not added his vote.

Sudden suspicion flowed into him. "To work, to work, my colleagues, my friends. We do not have time to waste!"

His happy words sent them all scattering to their tasks. Not one of them commented as he flew out into the clear air to claim a kite. He too had work to do, and they were all aware of it.

Right now, his work was to find Engineer Br'sei.

Br'sei glided around the side of the living highland. His bones tightened nervously, barely allowing him the lift he needed to fly, even down here in the thick air near the crust.

You are being ridiculous. He forced himself to relax and gained a little height. *You have grown things that are a thousand times more terrifying than these New People.*

But nothing stranger.

In truth, he was here only because Ambassador D'seun de-murred every single time Br'sei suggested they place close surveillance on the New People. D'seun worried about being seen, about the New People raising a peremptory challenge to their presence if they were seen. The ambassador seemed completely disinterested in the New People's explorations of the crust. Even now, when their activities had increased so markedly.

If the New People had a legitimate claim on this world, it could be disastrous, but it must be known. Br'sei listened to D'seun's stirring words through his headset and heard the en-thusiastic agreement of his colleagues. Grim silence settled within him. D'seun spoke, D'seun inspired, but D'seun did not know. Br'sei, on the other hand, had to know.

So Br'sei flitted around the highland, weaving in and out of its stony ripples to spy on the New People and see what could be seen.

Below him, Br'sei saw the flat, wing-shaped carriers that the New People used to take themselves from place to place. They had smooth hides and glistening windows and were un-believably clumsy. However, they seemed to serve their pur-pose well enough. Grace may have been sacrificed for durability.

No New People walked the surface between the transports. Perhaps they were dormant now. Br'sei dipped a little closer, equal parts of fear and excitement swelling his body.

Then, he saw movement on the ground. Two lumps of what he had first taken for crust moved toward the transports. From their shadow rose what looked like one of the People's own constructors.

Br'sei backwinged, holding his position and watching. The constructor and its accompanying tools glided between the transports as if sniffing at their sides, seeking what? He spoke to his headset, but it could pick up nothing from them, no exchange, no projection, nothing but silence.

At last, the tools retreated to a deep crevice in the highland wall. Br'sei dived after them, bunching himself up tightly to fit between the stone walls where they hid.

The tools made no move as he came within their perceptual range. Now he could see that the one was indeed a constructor. It had the umbrella, the deeply grooved cortex and the manipulator arms. The other two had only eyes and locomotors. Overseers? Recorders maybe?

"What is your purpose?" asked Br'sei in the most common command language.

No reply. Br'sei repeated the question in four of the other command languages he knew, also with no result.

Frustration tightened Br'sei's bones. "Who made your purpose? Engineer D'han? Engineer T'oth?" Neither name elicited any reaction. The tools stayed as they were, unmoving, unresponsive. Br'sei's crest ruffled. A tool should at least respond to its user's name. "Engineer P'tesk? Engineer—"

"Ambassador D'seun."

Startled, Br'sei's wings flapped on their own, lifting him and turning him. Ambassador D'seun flew over a ridge in the highland's wall and deflated until he was level with Br'sei and the tools.

"Good luck, Br'sei," said D'seun amiably. He spoke to the tools in a command language that Br'sei couldn't even recognize the roots of. The constructor touched the ambassador's headset. Br'sei realized with a start that he must be using a chemical link, something Br'sei hadn't seen in years.

"I would ask you what you're doing here, Br'sei," said the ambassador, "especially as this is Highland 76, not 45. But I imagine you feel you have the right to ask me that question first."

"I don't wish to presume, Ambassador." Br'sei sank diffidently. "But yes, I do wish to ask that question."

The constructor drifted away from Ambassador D'seun, who spoke another few words of his convoluted command language. The constructor headed back to the crevices of the highland with the two overseers crawling after it.

D'seun watched them go until the tools could no longer be told apart from the crust. "At the moment, the tools are monitoring the patterned radio wave transmissions between the New People and their transports, as well as their transports and their base." He swelled, just a little. "We need to refine our translation techniques. It still takes even our most adept engineers four or five dodec-hours to achieve what we think is an approximate translation of any given message."

Br'sei stared at the ambassador, framed there by the living highland. "It is difficult to accomplish such a work from a distance." He fought to keep his voice mild. "But you have said repeatedly that you do not want any tools within a mile of the New People, wherever they are."

Ambassador D'seun deflated slowly, as if he were too tired to keep his size and shape anymore. "I have wrestled with a great dilemma since we originally dropped the wind seeds onto this world, Br'sei. Now, you have the dubious honor of sharing it with me." He turned to face Br'sei. "But perhaps we should speak somewhere more comfortable?"

"If you wish, Ambassador." *Patience,* he told himself as his bones twitched. *The only way you're going to get your answers is by waiting him out.*

Br'sei had been helping to design the seeds for the candidate worlds when he first met D'seun. Br'sei was young for an adult, having been fully declared in his eightieth year.

Back then, there were still debates raging over what the nature of the seeding should be. Should it be a wide variety of organisms, both useful and strictly supportive, to make sure the candidate world would accept a range of life? Or should it be a single organism so that when it did begin to spread, there would be fewer interactions to calculate when the overlaying began?

Br'sei had been of the opinion that broad-seeding was the correct method, and his experiment house was working with two dozen different microcosms to show the differences in effect between broad-seeding and mono-seeding.

Then D'seun had flown up to the door without sending advance notice and asked for a tour and an appointment with Br'sei. Because D'seun was a speaker then, he got both.

The experiment house was an old, wise workplace with heavy screens and thick filters to keep its interior air absolutely sterile. Its cortices were complex and well grown, each able to monitor its crystalline microcosms for hours without supervision or correction, leaving the engineers free to work on projection and innovation.

Br'sei led D'seun from cosmos to cosmos, showing him the hardiness of the broad-seeding in the miniature ecosystems as opposed to the flimsy strains of mono-seeded cultures.

"The broad-seeding provides its own support system, you see, Speaker," said Br'sei as they paused to study yet another microcosm. The sphere's lensing sides allowed them to see through to the microscopic organisms thriving in the simulated cloud.

"Yes." D'seun pointed his muzzle at Br'sei. "But that is not truly the point, is it?"

Br'sei remembered how his crest had spread at those words. "Forgive me, Speaker, but that is the entire point."

"Forgive me, Engineer, but it is not," D'seun replied. "The point of the initial seeding is not to establish life, but merely to establish that life is a possibility. First we establish that life can exist on a world; then we survey that world carefully, understanding it thoroughly in its pure, prelife state. Then, and only then, can we start laying out the basis for a new canopy, one we design and supervise in its entirety." He turned his gaze back to the microcosm, deflating a little as he did. "We have acted too often without understanding. We must not do that with our new world. I fear we will have only one chance to make this plan of ours work."

Br'sei had felt himself swelling at that point, ready to argue, but the speaker's words flew ahead of his. "What I see here convinces me that you and yours have a tremendous understanding of how life can be built and layered. Your life-base designs are strong and rich." D'seun whistled, pleased. "I would like to talk to you about providing members for the initial teams, as well as engineers and designers for when New Home is found."

The implication that brushed against Br'sei was that this discussion would take place only if Br'sei agreed to the idea of a mono-seeding. The speaker did make several excellent points, and the idea of Br'sei and his own team working on the foundations of New Home was a powerful lure.

"I think I could be convinced, Speaker," Br'sei admitted, fanning his wings gently to keep himself close to D'seun. "Let me bring some of my engineers, and let us discuss this. Some new microcosms may need to be designed."

"Thank you, Engineer Br'sei," said D'seun, and the words sank deeply into Br'sei's skin. "Bring your people. Let us think about what we may do together."

In the end, with Br'sei's help, D'seun had triumphed. As a result, Br'sei and his team, which he picked out with D'seun's help, were given the most promising world to seed with a mono-culture of their own design.

It had worked and here they were, with D'seun as ambassador and Br'sei as collaborator.

Br'sei's wings faltered slightly as that thought filtered through him.

"I have been thinking, Engineer Br'sei." D'seun banked into an updraft. The warm air from the highland with its delicate taste of life lifted him high. "We say 'Life spreads life' all the time, but we do not ever hold still long enough to think what that should really mean."

"Should mean?" Br'sei's crest ruffled and spread flat, helping him keep an even path in the turbulent wind from the highlands. Pockets of heat and cold bumped against him, making him have to work to keep his position steady relative to the ambassador. If he was not careful, he would be trapped by the same eloquent arguments D'seun had used on the youngsters. "Not 'does mean'?"

"On Home, I would have said 'does mean.'" The updraft spilled D'seun into the cooler air and he drifted down again until he was level with Br'sei. "But here we are dealing with new possibilities. Here we can say 'should mean.'"

Br'sei deflated just a little. The ambassador's words were like a storm wind. They could sweep you along to an unknown destination before you even realized you were in a current too strong for you to fight.

"And have you decided what 'Life spreads life' should mean, Ambassador?"

"Not yet." D'seun cupped his wings and hovered in place in a relative calm. "But I am wondering if it involves surrounding yourself with things that do not live."

"What?" The single word burst out of Br'sei before he could even think about what he said.

D'seun dipped his muzzle. "Their transports, their base, they do not live. They are metal and ceramic without any living component I can find, and I have looked carefully."

"But that's . . ." Br'sei searched for a strong enough word and found nothing. He gathered his thoughts again. "They are other. Their life is different from ours," he said, trying to give his words weight, but all the time he was thinking, *Their home does not live? How can it care for them? How can they care for it?*

D'seun glided close to him. "The question is, are they life we can live with?"

Br'sei deflated reflexively as the last sentence touched his muzzle. "Do you think they are insane, Ambassador?" Insanity was the gravest accusation that could be made against another being, worse than greed, worse than jealousy. Insanity meant they would ravage the life around them and that they would have to be stopped before they could damage the larger balance.

D'seun's bones bunched tightly and he sank. "I don't know, Engineer. I do know they frighten me."

"Then why—"

D'seun's teeth clacked but his amusement was grim. "Then why did I fight so hard for this world? Because this is the world where our life can exist, Br'sei. The only one we have ever found where it can."

Their home does not live. Br'sei rolled his eyes upward, as if he thought to see the New People's base floating overhead, drawn by the thought. The New People had not been his study or concern. His time had been spent with the highlands, the clouds, and the wind seeds. Even so, someone in the team should have told him about this.

Unless an ambassador told them not to. . . . But that was too much even for Br'sei, and he did not struggle when his thoughts swerved back to the New People. *Do they isolate themselves from life, or do they just need to isolate their kind of life? How can we know?*

"I have worked hard to keep this knowledge quiet, Engineer Br'sei," said D'seun, as if he read Br'sei's thoughts. "There are those who would take the facts of how the New People live and create a panic to spread across all the winds of Home. Ambassador T'sha, to begin with."

Br'sei shook himself. "Do you have so little faith in your colleagues, Ambassador?" he asked, being deliberately blunt.

"No." D'seun swelled. "I have so much experience with them. T'sha is rich. She hands out promises as if they were guesting gifts. She does not want this world for New Home because of the New People. I have managed to block her so far, but what if she were able to cry insanity?" A single beat of his wings brought him towering over Br'sei. "Would any of the People be willing to run from insanity toward insanity?" Now their muzzles touched and the ambassador's words sank deep into Br'sei's skin. "How long does Home have left for us, Br'sei? Twenty years? Forty? How long will it take before a new world can support us in all our billions?"

"At least fifty years," admitted Br'sei.

"So, we have no time to waste in panic and argument."

"But—"

"But if the New People are insane, they must be treated as such." D'seun let himself drift away. "If they are not, they must be treated as such. Right now, we know only three things—that they have no legitimate claim on this world, that we cannot decide on their sanity until we understand them better, and that we cannot waste time looking for yet another candidate world."

Br'sei's bones bunched together. He would have plummeted had not the warm plumes from the highland cradled him. "I am not so sure, Ambassador."

D'seun dipped his muzzle. "Of course not. These are not small thoughts. This must all be digested and studied from all angles. But tell me this: you do truly agree that action without knowledge will lead to disaster?"

"It can," admitted Br'sei.

"And you do agree that we have no time to waste in the creation of New Home?"

Br'sei dipped his muzzle. "I have seen the cities rotting too,

Ambassador. I heard your tale of Gaith. I am aware our time is short."

"Good." D'seun flew over him, letting his hands graze against Br'sei's crest. "Then give me this much. Do not panic Ambassador T'sha when she comes. Do not tell her how much we know." He turned on a wingtip. "And help me understand the New People. With knowledge, your doubts and mine will all be resolved. We will not be fumbling and flapping in our helplessness, as we must on Home, where the diseases and their progeny have flown too far ahead for us to ever understand, let alone overtake. Here, we must always know how to proceed."

We must always know how to proceed. Br'sei let D'seun's words echo inside him. He wanted to believe that was possible, but sometimes he doubted it. What he did know, however, was that D'seun had convinced himself of the rightness of his words, and a mere engineer would not change Ambassador D'seun's mind.

Ambassador T'sha, however, might be able to, and if she couldn't change D'seun's mind, she might be able to sway the Law Meet, which even D'seun could not ignore.

But Br'sei would have to steer a careful path. If D'seun did not think Br'sei was convinced, the ambassador would find a way to have him removed from the team. That was very much D'seun's way.

"I shall work with you, Ambassador." Br'sei inflated himself until his size was equal with D'seun's. "Together we will see what we can find."

I do not, however, promise you will like what I will do with what we find.

It was not until they had returned to the base and dispersed to their separate tasks that Br'sei realized D'seun had never answered one question about the tools near the New People.

CHAPTER FIVE

A fresh United Nations flag dominated the rear wall of the passenger clearing area. Its sky blue background made a stark contrast to the soft, shifting reds and golds that the walls had been set for. Ben was glad to see, however, that Helen had drawn the line at welcoming banners.

Ben stood beside Helen and Michael. The assorted Veneran department heads ranged past them in a ragged line. Beyond the hatch, they could hear the soft whirs and bumps of the docking corridor extending and clamping itself to the newly arrived shuttle.

"Here they come," announced Tori from the control booth.

"The intercom better be off in the corridor," muttered Helen.

"Tori knows what she's doing," Michael assured her, somewhat absently.

Ben said nothing. He was too busy dealing with his own emotions. Anger, irrational and completely out of proportion, seethed inside him. He feared that if he had to open his mouth, it would all come spilling out in an unstoppable red flood.

God, I knew it was going to be bad, but I didn't expect it to be this bad.

The last time he'd seen the U.N. come into a colony, he'd been in a holding cell, watching lines of neatly dressed judges and bureaucrats arrive with their armed escorts. There seemed to be hundreds of them, all there to deal with the "criminals" who had "broken the rule of law in Bradbury." He remembered the fear he'd felt, wondering what would happen to them all now, and the deep shame at that fear.

None of the people standing next to him now knew about that cell or that he had ever lived on Bradbury at all. He'd managed to disconnect his records from that past and that person. But he could not disconnect his memories, even if there were times he wanted to.

Like now.

The hatch cranked itself open. Ben's stomach clenched itself involuntarily. *Get over it! They're just tourists. They're going to be rumpled and gravity dizzy and slightly stupid, like any other crowd of Earthlings.*

Edmund Waicek, the man Ben considered to be the most dangerous member of the C.A.C., had cheerfully sent Venera's governing board a list of their invaders. Ben had to admit, Helen had worked her end quite well. It could have been a lot worse.

The first two down the ramp Ben recognized as Robert Stykos and Terry Wray, the media faces. Their job was to create the in-stream "news" presentations on the U.N. investigation of the Discovery. Both had been restructured to look exactly average, only more beautiful. They might have been brother and sister, with their coffee-and-cream skin, big brown eyes, and shoulder-length black hair (hers pinned under a bronze scarf, his pulled back into a ponytail under a red beaded cap). But where Stykos was tall and broad, Wray was petite, almost elfin. Both wore glittering camera bands on their foreheads and command bracelets on their wrists.

"Mr. Stykos, Ms. Wray." Helen, in full public relations

mode, stepped forward and shook their hands. "Welcome to Venera Base. I'm Dr. Helen Failia. Allow me to introduce my associate, Dr. Bennet Godwin, who is our head of personnel and chief volcanologist. . . ."

So it began. Stykos and Wray both looked long and hard at him, making sure their cameras got a good image of him smiling and shaking their soft hands. Lindi Manzur, the architect, beamed up at him as if she'd never met anyone more fascinating, except maybe Troy Peachman (was that a real name?), the comparative culturalist (whatever that was), at whom she kept glancing fondly as he followed her down the line, shaking everybody's hands with a kind of firm enthusiasm that came with practice.

What have you two been doing for the past week and a half? he wondered snidely.

After them came Julia Lott, the archeologist, a sturdy fireplug of a woman with a square face and tired eyes. She was followed by Isaac Walters who looked so uncomfortable that Ben had to wonder if he'd ever left Mother Earth before.

Out of the corner of his eye, Ben saw Grace Meyer smile broadly and step forward from the line.

Oh, right, this is the biologist, he thought as he passed Walters down to Michael.

Next, a tall, pale woman in artistic black and white swept up the line. Veronica Hatch, here to look at the laser and pronounce judgment. In contrast to Walters, she seemed ready to parachute down to the ground and start digging in.

There was a pause then, just long enough for Ben's anger to start simmering again. There were only two people left to come.

Angela Cleary and Philip Bowerman emerged together from the docking corridor. She had sandy skin and sandy hair, which she wore short under her white scarf. He was darker, with wavy hair and tropical skin and eyes that took in the entire room at a glance. Both of them were tall, broad in the shoulders and narrow at the waist, people whose bulk came not from body-mod, but from work. They both wore the blue tunics with white collars that were the uniform of U.N. security assessors on official duty.

Ben's blood ran hot, then cold. It must have showed in his face. He knew Michael was looking at him, but he couldn't help it. He'd sat for hours in little windowless rooms with uniforms like these, being recorded and interrogated until he couldn't think straight, couldn't remember if he'd implicated his friends or not, couldn't decide whether his own lies still made sense. All he could do was feel his burning eyes, raw throat, and aching bladder.

What if they know me? What if they were there? The thought rose unbidden from the back of his brain.

"Pleased to meet you, Dr. Godwin," Cleary was saying. Ben focused on her, a little startled, but she just smiled politely.

Ben stuck his hand out and shook hers. It was strong and slightly calloused. He made himself look into her amber-colored eyes. He saw no hint of recognition there, and relief, as irrational and unlooked for as his anger and his fear, almost robbed him of his balance.

"Pleased to meet you, Ms. Cleary," he answered in as steady a voice as he could manage. *Too young,* he thought to himself. *Security has limits on how rejuvenated you can be, and they're both way too young to have been at Bradbury.*

That realization allowed him to greet Bowerman with something approaching equanimity.

Then, it was over. The yewners mingled with the department heads, making polite small talk about their voyage and the base. Helen flitted between the conversational groups, reminding everyone of the reception scheduled for that evening. Grace Meyer walked Isaac Walters a little way off from the general crowd and talked to him in low, urgent tones. Michael took charge of Cleary and Bowerman and was telling them about the provisions he'd made to get them access to base records regarding the Discovery. Stykos and Wray stood back and photographed it all.

Then, in groups of twos and threes, the yewners and their chaperones began to make their way to the elevator bundles. The crowd thinned, and Ben found he could breathe again.

The sound of footsteps echoing through the docking corridor turned Ben around again. Another person emerged. This one wore a tan tunic and trousers with blue ID patches, the standard uniform for crews on distance ships. It took Ben a moment to recognize him.

"Hello, Dr. Godwin."

Joshua Kenyon, one of Venera's atmospheric researchers, held out his hand. Well, no, he wasn't exactly Venera's. He'd never made the commitment to live on the base. He just came up every now and again to do his work on Rayleigh scattering in the upper atmosphere and then went back down to Mother Earth to analyze and publish what he'd found. Because of that, Ben found himself unable to really like the man.

Kenyon was also not scheduled to be back for at least another six months.

"Hello, Dr. Kenyon." Ben shook his hand. "This is unexpected, especially in uniform."

Kenyon blushed a little. "I know. They weren't even going to let me back up. Special flight for U.N. VIPs only. But I knew a couple of guys on the crew, and they kind of smuggled me in." He gestured at his uniform. "Not to spec, I know, but when I heard about the Discovery, I couldn't help myself. I'm really hoping Dr. Failia will let me get a look at that laser."

Of course. Kenyon used lasers constantly in his work. Ben's dislike for the man did not change the fact that Kenyon was probably one of the best optical engineers Venera had access to. Of course he wanted a look at the laser. He'd be just the person to pull the machine apart and see what it was made of and what it was for.

Ben shook his head regretfully. "I'm sorry. Helen's put a ban on any Venerans, or anyone else, going down there until the yewners . . . the U.N. team has finished up. Doesn't want anybody to get in their way or to challenge whatever theories they come up with by presenting a whole bunch of facts. She says there'll be plenty of time for that later."

Kenyon's face fell one muscle at a time. "I may just ask her anyway," he said at last. "Do you think getting on my knees and begging would help any?"

Ben did not laugh. "She's got her hands full, Dr. Kenyon. I think it'd be better if you just waited until the investigative team's finished."

Kenyon's eyes searched Ben's face, and Ben saw in them the knowledge of his, Ben's, personal dislike. That was all right; he'd never supposed it to be a secret.

At last, Kenyon blew out a sigh. "Okay, if that's the way it is, that's the way it is. I'll wait." He paused. "Or did you rent out my room while I was gone?"

"No, your quarters are still right where you left them." Venera kept a set of apartments for people like Kenyon who came and went on regular schedules. Ben stepped aside. "Sorry you went through all this for nothing."

The thought *no you're not,* flickered across Kenyon's face, but he quickly smoothed it out. "Thanks," he said as he strode past Ben, heading for the elevators.

Alone, Ben let his shoulders sag. The U.N. flag fluttered in the breeze from the ventilator shafts, and Ben found his hands itching to go over and rip it down.

Pull it together. You have more important things to worry about.

Ben focused his eyes on the corridor and marched past the flag, almost as if it wasn't there.

The door to the Surveyors' lab opened as soon as it identified Bennet Godwin, just as all the doors on Venera did. That fact could still amaze him. There had been a point when he assumed he'd never be trusted again.

And I may be about to blow all of it. He shoved the thought aside. This was not some petty academic political battle. This one was for the real world.

Except for Derek Cusmanos and several dozen neatly arrayed survey drones, the cavernous room was empty. All the personnel who'd been assigned to Derek were off either in the scarabs or in their own offices, poring over years of satellite data, looking for more alien bases. The mammoth wall screens showed a series of seemingly random still shots—the mushroomlike dome of a pancake volcano, the ripples of one of the lava deltas, the ragged, concentric rings of a collapsed crater.

Derek himself crouched in front of one of his drones. This was one of the surface surveyors, which looked like miniature scarabs with eyes and arms. Derek had it turned over on its side so he could get at the hatch in its belly. Whatever he saw there was so absorbing that he did not look up as Ben started across the floor.

"Derek?"

Derek grunted and held up one finger. Ben stopped where he was, folding his hands behind his back and getting ready to wait. Derek, like most of the mechanical engineers Ben knew, had the tendency to get completely absorbed in his work. Ben studied the rows of drones with their spindly arms, picks and containers for taking samples, lasers for measuring, cameras for every kind of photography. Derek knew them all. Had built half of them. Had come very close to losing his job because no one felt the need to fund a human mapmaker when drones and computers could do that just fine. The drones themselves could, of course, be cared for by the same staff that took care of the scarabs.

Derek finished his repairs or adjustments, closed the hatch, and heaved the drone upright onto its treads. Only then did he stand up and really acknowledge Ben's presence.

"Afternoon, Dr. Godwin." Derek plucked a sterile towel out of the box and started wiping his hands with it. "What can I do for you?"

"Afternoon." Derek had been one of Ben's students when he was still teaching. Ben had long ago given up trying to get the younger man to use his first name. "Have you got the new pictures of Ozza Mons?"

"Fresh in." Derek tossed the towel down the recycling shaft and plunked himself behind the sprawling, semicircular desk that was in his main workstation. The desk woke up, and he typed in a quick command sequence. The wall image of the lava delta disappeared, replaced by the ragged, ashen gray throat of an old, massive volcano. "Looks pretty dead."

"May just be dormant." Ben studied the picture, but the familiar sense of excitement failed to rise in him. "We'll have to go down and look at it."

"If you can get a scarab for anything but ogling the Discovery." Derek shook his head at his keyboard. "It's amazing, you know? I mean, I knew, once we found it, that the Terrans wouldn't think there was anything else worthwhile up here, but I thought the Board . . ." He stopped.

Ben held up his hand. "Now that the tourists are here, everybody's supposed to go back to their normal duties. Dr. Failia wants to give your visitors plenty of room to play."

Derek made a sour face. Ben returned a smile and changed the subject. "Have you found anything that looks like another outpost?"

Derek shook his head. "They've given me the entire geology department, and we've got every surveyor, from the satellites to the minirovers, set on fine-tooth comb, but there's nothing."

"Think we will find anything?"

Derek started but recovered quickly. "How would I know?"

Ben shrugged. "You found the first one. I thought you might recognize . . . traces."

Derek didn't look at him. His gaze wandered over the silent ranks of surveyors with their waldos, cameras, and caterpillar treads. They were heavy, blocky, reinforced things, completely unlike the delicate machines Ben had worked with on Mars. "The drones found the first one, Dr. Godwin, not me. But there are no traces of anything around it. It's just sitting there, a random occurrence." He paused and finally returned his gaze to Ben. "Or have your people found something new?"

Ben barked out a laugh. "You have all my people. You're going to hear anything long before I do." Then, he paused, as if considering a new thought. "Although . . . well, you've got a trained eye. Can I get you to take a look at one of the new batches of images your team passed me?"

"Sure." Derek poised his hands over the command board.

"It's file number AT-3642."

Derek entered the number and brought up the picture on the wall screen. It was a black-and-white still shot, taken from one of their ancient satellites. It showed a gray raised ring with a dark center and long pale ridges radiating from the sides. Derek studied it for a moment.

Ben leaned one hand against the back of Derek's chair and peered at the image, as if trying to see it in greater detail.

"Looks like a tick," Derek said. A tick was a type of volcano found only on Venus. It got its name because from above it looked like a gigantic, round-bodied insect with its crooked legs sticking out at irregular angles.

"Yeah, it does," said Ben, watching Derek carefully. "Except it's never been mapped."

"Oh? Well, that describes a lot of the planet." Venus had three times the land area of Earth. Detailed mapping was the work of multiple lifetimes. "Do you want me to put it on the list for close study?"

"No, no." Ben shook his head. *Especially since it does seem you've never seen it before.* "You've got your hands full. Just see about routing me a couple of close-ups during the next flyover, okay?"

"Okay." Derek made a note on one of his flat screens. "Was there anything else?"

"Not really." Ben straightened up. "Will I see you at the reception?"

"Maybe." Derek turned his attention back to his command board. The lava delta reappeared on the wall, this time with the white lines of a measuring grid laid over it. "When I'm done here."

"You should consider putting in an appearance," Ben suggested with a small smile. "I think Grandma Helen is counting noses. If she isn't, she'll be reviewing the tapes later."

Derek glanced up. "Thanks, Dr. Godwin. I'll show myself."

"Good choice." He patted the boy on the shoulder and showed himself out.

Ben walked down the broad corridor to the elevator bays and, as was his habit, took the sweeping staircase instead. Space was Venera's one true luxury, and Ben had to admit he reveled in it. The stairs were wide, and the ceilings were high. There was room for people coming up, going down, and just standing around talking or leaning against the outer railing. The elevator shafts made mini-atriums, so he could look the whole, long, dizzy way down and up again and hear the sounds of purposeful life drifting to him from each of the twenty-four decks. Ten thousand people living and working peacefully together. It could be paradise if it were allowed to be.

Ben turned off at the landing for the administration level, getting ready to head for his office. But he stopped in mid-stride and glanced at the clock on the wall. Quarter of five, with the reception at six. No one would think anything of it if he didn't stay at his desk until the required hour.

And what Ben really wanted to do could not be done in the office.

So he returned to the stairs and walked down three levels to the residential section. The apartments took up most of the two levels above the farm and one level below. Everyone had a full suite of rooms: bed, bath, study, living, and kitchen. Even the visitors. With the soaring ceilings, full-spectrum lights, and generous use of e-windows and greenery, you could almost forget you were in a colony.

In his own rooms, Ben always kept one of his screens set to show the clouds outside. He did not want to forget.

Other than that, Ben's apartment was pretty much as he had moved into it. Someone looking for evidence of the owner's personality would have had to work hard. After a while, they might have picked out the shiny chunk of obsidian on the end table by the couch, the brightly polished garnet on the half-wall that divided the kitchen from the living room, and the piles of open screen rolls on the desk, coffee table, and couch. From this they could have concluded that the owner liked rocks and was dedicated to his work.

As his door shut behind him, Ben crossed to the sofa. He picked up a pile of screen rolls to clear space for himself and sat down. His briefcase rested on the coffee table. He didn't jack it in; he just woke it and called up a privately encrypted file that waited for both the password and the scan of his fingertips from the command board.

The file opened for him and displayed a picture identical to Derek's AT-3642.

It did look like a tick. It had the circular center and the ridges radiating out like crooked legs. In black and white and two dimensions, those ridges appeared to be level with the ground—until you had spent a day looking at everything you had as if they were alien artifacts because you couldn't help yourself, until you enlarged it and refined it and squinted at it for hours.

Then you saw it was not level with the ground, that the ring was, in fact, sitting well above ground level, and that the "ridges" might be supports of some kind.

He couldn't be sure, of course. The only way to be sure would be to fly one of Derek's prize camera drones in there, shine a laser over the thing, and make a holograph of it. But close study of anything on Venera involved other people—assistants and their supervisors, Derek as the drone keeper; Helen, who had to know what was going on at all times. Ben did not want anyone, *anyone,* else involved in this yet. Anyone on Venera anyway.

What Ben knew currently was that this object was approximately 1.3 kilometers across and that it had been there somewhere between 40 and 170 years. The *Magellan* probe sent up in the 1990s hadn't seen it, but the *Francis Drake* had, and the *Francis Drake* went up just as the first plates of Venera were being bolted together.

So never mind where the Discovery with its three little holes in the ground came from. Where did this . . . *thing* come from?

But no one was looking at it, except him. Derek's complete nonrecognition had told him that. If someone else had been checking out this spot or this object, Derek would have confirmed it. Everyone else was looking in the ground for more holes. No one had looked up.

Ben's first thought had been to rush to Helen with this, but he'd hesitated. He told himself that it was just because he wanted to be sure. He didn't want to speak before he had the facts.

But that wasn't it, and even as he was rationalizing his actions at three in the morning, he knew that.

Ben slumped backward and ran his hand over his scalp, scrubbing the gray bristles that were all that was left of his hair. Male-pattern baldness he'd never bothered to get corrected. He hated med-trips when they were necessary, never mind the idea of getting stuck in one of the capsules for cosmetic touch-ups.

He'd had a full head of chestnut hair at Bradbury. He'd been so young. Ben chuckled to himself. *God, when did twenty-seven get to be young?*

He'd taken his own sweet time getting through college. Some of his friends joked he was in on the "eternity program." Ben replied he was just looking for something to get excited about. Comparative planetology, with its possibilities for exploration and discovery, had come close to filling the bill.

Then he went to Bradbury for his post-doc work and he found the real thing.

Theodore Fuller was just picking up steam when Ben arrived. No one on Earth took him seriously, but in the colony itself, that was another story. The stream was full of his words and of people talking about them.

Ben had arrived at Arestech, Inc., to set up shop in their lab and run their surveyors with every intention of ignoring Fuller's message. But he couldn't help hearing. To his surprise, Fuller didn't talk about the good old days of the nation states, like most people who had grief with the U.N. did. He didn't talk about the past at all. Instead he talked with enthusiasm and delight about the present—how modern technology had finally made possible a truly free flow of information, information available to each and every human being no matter who they were, no matter where they were. Information made it possible for everyone to control their own lives completely in a way that had never been possible before. It could bring them into contact with whomever and whatever they needed. They could pick and choose what their lives held. There was no more need for middlemen or for central government.

After all, what did governments do? Provide security? There were no more nations to wage war on each other. Personal security could be provided by electronics or a private company, depending on the needs and desires of the individual. The government regulated commerce? Why? The market, like nature, could take care of itself and had for a long time now. When was the last real economic collapse? Late twenty-first century, wasn't it? Before the stream was truly established.

How about rule of law? Employment for lawyers and bureaucrats mostly. A person who felt unjustly treated could seek satisfaction in courts run on the same principles as any other business. The ones in which the arbitration and settlement procedures were seen as just and fair would have the most subscribers and work with the greatest number of private security companies. Those who didn't like the justice of one system could subscribe to another which they read about and evaluated in-stream.

The central government did not need to exist. It was an idea from previous centuries. It was like the great North American weed called kudzu. It had invaded so long ago no one remembered where it came from. They just knew it was there, and they spent a lot of time, effort, and money dealing with it because no one knew how to get rid of it. No, because no one was ready to do what was necessary to get rid of it.

Well, the good news was that dealing with the U.N. was a lot easier than dealing with kudzu. All you had to do to get rid of government was say no. Simple. Direct. Say no, show the bureaucrats the nearest ship out, and get on with your life. Your life, your money, your future. Yours. No one to say who could and could not build on the planets, no endless rounds of licensing for ships and shipping, no one to hedge or ban scientific research that frightened them, no one to ever again supervise bloodbaths like the U.S. Disarmament.

Ben had had no blaze-of-light revelation. He'd started reading because he almost couldn't help himself. Fuller and Fuller's ideas were all anybody talked about. He had to find out for himself whether they would work or not.

The answer shocked and scared him. It could work. The free flow of information was the key, just as Fuller said. The U.N. had been, in some ways, a necessary stage to eliminate the barriers imposed by nation states and national currency. But now that it had nothing external to fight against, it had turned around, like all powerful governments had throughout history, and started to feed on its own, and people put up with it because they couldn't see any way past it.

Bradbury and its people could show them. Bradbury could push the U.N. out the door and thrive. When they did, the rest of the worlds would see that it could be done, and done safely and quickly. It would start with Mars, out on the frontier, but it would spread all the way back down to Mother Earth herself.

It should have worked, but they moved too fast. Fuller got bad advice, or maybe he just got overconfident, but they overestimated the number of their followers in Bradbury. Too many people just stood around and did nothing. Too many other people actively tried to undermine the revolution and were judged dangerous to the implementation of the new system. Transporting all the dissenters back to Earth turned out to be a bigger problem than had been anticipated. During the process of transportation, someone got sloppy and didn't run safety checks on all the ships that carried the dissenters away.

Then there were the ones who misunderstood what was happening and decided to take charge in their own way before the security systems could be established. Revenge had overwhelmed the fragile court corporations.

None of that changed the basic principles. Fuller's ideas still held. But twenty years had passed and no one else had found the time or the place to put them into practice.

Until now.

Ben stared at the clouds displayed on his view screen. They billowed and boiled, filling the world outside. Even after so long, they could still be awe inspiring.

When he'd first stood inside the Discovery, his thoughts had tumbled over each other, almost too fast for him to follow. Awe, fear, wonder, humility, and then, slowly, almost shamefully, came the idea that he might be able to use this great thing that had happened. This might be the catalyst for the shift in thinking that would be needed to finish what Ted Fuller had started.

The more he thought, the more he saw and uncovered on his own, the more certain he became. This was it. It just had to be managed, that was all. Not suppressed, not lied about, just managed. Everything could be made to work out for the best for all the worlds, including Venus, if they just moved carefully.

Well? He tapped his fingers restlessly against his thigh. *If you're going to do it, do it. If not, put your file away and go get dressed up for the yewners.*

Ben leaned forward and jacked the case into the table. He set up a quick search code, attached his best encryption to it, and dropped it into the queue for the next com burst to Earth. Then he got up to shave and change for the reception.

One of the features of the stream that few people bothered to take notice of was that if you constructed your packet correctly, you did not actually have to store your information anywhere. So many different, completely untended machines were constantly receiving and rerouting data that it was possible to keep a packet bouncing between them. Ben had several packets that had been flying from relay to relay for twenty years now. He'd lost three to badly timed hardware upgrades that he'd failed to get wind of, but other than that, his most secret information bounced happily around the solar system, untraceable, not only because of its encryptions, but because it seldom landed anywhere long enough for any one machine to make a complete record of its contents.

The disadvantage of this was that it took awhile to find the packet, once you did go looking for it.

Ben returned to his case, clean shaven and dressed in tunic and trousers of a suitably conservative blue-gray. A matching cap with black beading covered his head. He checked the screen display.

Success.

His searcher had recovered the packet in one of the repeater relays between Earth and the Moon and had rerouted it back to Venus. Ben accessed his four-tier decryption key and added the password.

The packet opened to display the face of an aging man with dark hair, pale skin, a suggestion of a beard, and mud-brown eyes under heavy brows. His name was Paul Mabrey. He had assorted degrees from assorted universities. He worked as a risk assessor for various small companies, spending his time traveling from colony to colony, mostly on Mars, looking at new market niches and good suppliers. He took med-trips and vacations back on Mother Earth regularly but not excessively.

He had been in Bradbury during the rebellion, and while it was felt that he had some sympathies toward Fuller's faction, surveillance on him had been turned off over fifteen years ago because he never did anything remotely suspicious.

He was, in fact, the man Ben used to be.

Once upon a time, Ben, then called Paul Mabrey, had been dismissed by the yewners who had taken over Bradbury as being of little consequence. They did, however, post automatic surveillance over him, as they did every rebel, just in case. For three years, Paul behaved himself meekly, like a good defeated puppy. He watched his friends jailed, watched Fuller hauled back to Earth for trial and incarceration. He watched the yewners take up posts on every street corner and randomly search the passersby. He watched the taxes go up and the licenses go down and travel get restricted. He sat in his apartment at night and hated himself because there was nothing he could do, not now, not ever again, because the yewners would never really take their eyes off him. The free flow of information that Fuller had touted as the route to the future would make it impossible for him to hide.

He had one thing left to him. The yewners had not quite uncovered the extent of what Paul had done for Fuller. He'd specialized in helping make clip-outs—in-stream ghosts of people who wound up on various payrolls and mailing lists and who, eventually, wound up with various levels of access and permission to various segments of the communications networks. When the uprising came, those clip-outs gave the software corruption teams that Paul was a part of a handle on the U.N. networks, which he used to shut them down.

Minor stuff, really, a low-level hacker trick.

But what he labored over at night, almost every night, was not. It was researched and tested, a little bit here, a little bit there. It was years of learning under Fuller's best, a few minor bribes, a couple of slow, painful system break-ins, and a whole lot of patience.

Then, Paul received notice that his surveillance period was up and he was declared rehabilitated. Good luck to you, Mr. Mabrey.

Paul, grimly satisfied, had closed the letter and gone in-stream to request permission politely to travel to Giant Leap on business. The yewner bureaucrat on the other end was in a benevolent mood that day and let him go.

Two weeks later, Paul Mabrey left for Luna. He arrived at Giant Leap and stayed for three months, working on various consulting jobs and contracts. Then—according to all available records, anyway—Paul Mabrey went home.

That same day, a man named Bennet Godwin, who had—according to all available records—arrived in Giant Leap on Luna from the Republic of Manhattan space port, got a job as a geologist for Dorson Mines, Inc.

No one knew how many clip-outs floated around the stream. Usually they were used by people wishing to perpetrate some kind of fraud. They were vague constructs, tied to a few vital records and easily torn apart or scared away by semideterminedscrutiny.

A very few were like Paul, who sat in-stream and stared at Ben out of eyes that could have been his own. Paul had been nurtured and cared for. He had aged as Ben had aged. He had subscriptions to the major news services and joined in-stream discussions on various items of interest. He had credit accounts, and he used them. He drew pay from companies he consulted for. He vacationed, theatered, and kept apartments in Giant Leap and Burroughs. He even had personal contact codes, which a simulation would answer and alert Ben when they were used.

Now, it was time for Paul to come back to life. Paul was going to get hold of some very interesting information and pass it along to a few old associates. Paul still had a few tricks up his sleeve to keep the yewners from noticing he'd revived some acquaintances that were still, after all those years, under surveillance and travel restrictions.

Paul still had a chance to prove he was not useless.

Ben, heedless of the time, hunched over his briefcase and started typing.

". . . with mutual cooperation and free exchange of ideas we will together unravel this, the greatest of human mysteries."

Vee applauded politely, along with the rest of the gathering. Dr. Failia smiled and stepped out from behind the podium, shifting immediately from solemn speech-giver to smiling greeter-of-friends-and-strangers. Vee found herself grinning. The speeches had been well delivered and short, the food was good, and the view . . . the view was stunning.

Vee hadn't stood in Venera's observation hall for eight years. She had forgotten the impact of being surrounded by the huge, constantly shifting landscapes of gray, white, and gold created by the clouds. Observation Hall was ringed, from the white floor to domed ceiling, with a seamless window of industrial quartz, so it was possible to stand and stare until you felt as if you were alone and exposed in the midst of that boiling alien mist.

Not that that's going to happen tonight. Vee felt her mouth quirk up. *The place is way too full.*

A couple of hundred Venerans plus the investigative team circulated around tables loaded with appropriate predinner snacks and beverages. Stykos and Wray, camera bands firmly in place, flanked the tall dark woman who Vee vaguely remembered was head of meteorology. Lindi Manzur stood in front of the window, a little too close to Troy Peachman, who was gesturing grandly as he expounded about something. Vee smiled softly and turned away from their private moment.

Everyone in the gathering had made an effort to show some gold or silk. Vee herself had been torn between wanting to put on a good show for the cameras and not wanting to break the conservative veneer she'd been carefully cultivating during the entire week-and-a-half flight up here.

In the end, she'd selected a green-and-gold paneled skirt, with a green jacket trimmed with gold piping and an abbreviated gold turban with a green veil falling down behind to cover her unbound hair. It looked good enough to make the story cut, but not so outrageous as to offend academic sensibility.

Apparently, however, she was not circulating enough. Out of the corner of her eye, Vee saw Dr. Failia making a beeline for her.

"Good evening, Dr. Hatch. Thank you for coming."

Vee shook her hand. "I'm sorry I'm late, Dr. Failia. I'd forgotten just how big Venera is."

"After a week on a ship, it can take some getting used to, yes." Dr. Failia nodded sympathetically. "Tell me, did you have a chance to review the visuals we've taken of the Discovery?"

"Yes, in between learning how not to get squashed and burned when we go down." Vee smiled to let Dr. Failia know she was kidding.

Dr. Failia laughed once, politely. "And did you form any initial plans as to how to proceed?"

"Yes. The first thing we need is a spectrographic analysis, to find out what kind of laser we're dealing with." Vee warmed as she talked, excited about the possibilities her research might open. "Then, I think . . ." Vee's gaze strayed over Dr. Failia's shoulder. Michael Lum, the security chief, waited two steps behind her.

Dr. Failia followed her gaze. "Excuse me, Dr. Hatch," she said hastily. "Please, help yourself to the buffet."

Dr. Failia crossed quickly to Lum, who murmured something in her ear. They both looked up at the entranceway, just as Bennet Godwin walked through. Failia frowned and strode over to the latecomer.

Uh-oh, Vee turned away and skirted the conversational knots as she made her way to the food tables. *Somebody's getting demerits for tardiness.*

The buffet was a good spread, with the Western traditional cheese and crackers, but also with couscous, falafel, and various flat breads, triangles of toast with what looked like mushroom paté, miniature empeñadas, and some blue pastry things that Vee, with all her experience of artsy receptions, couldn't put a name to. Glasses of wine flanked bowls of ginger and fruit punches, as well as silver samovars of tea and coffee.

Vee was debating over what to sample next, when she felt someone walking up to her side.

"Excuse me. Are you Dr. Veronica Hatch?"

Vee turned to face a sparsely built man with ruddy skin and tawny eyes. He was only a few centimeters taller than she was. He wore a blue baseball cap over his thick brown hair instead of a more fashionable brimless cap or half-turban. It made a pleasantly rebellious contrast to his formal gold-and-black tunic and trousers. Vee decided she liked him.

"That's what they tell me," Vee answered cheerfully and extended her hand. "Hi."

"Hi." He shook her hand with a good grip, which was also pleasant. Most people got a look at her long, thin hand and adjusted their greeting touch to something overly delicate. "I'm Joshua Kenyon. Josh."

Ah. His name rang memory chimes inside Vee and brought up the titles of several recently surveyed publications. "Vee. I've read you."

He did not, to his credit, look at all surprised. Dr. Kenyon had about a gigabyte of published work on tracking particle flow and interaction in the Venusian atmosphere using real-time laser holography techniques. Vee's job, before she got her first patent and turned to experiential holograms, was "time-resolved sequential holographic particle imaging velocimetry," which was the official way of saying she took four-dimensional images of particles in dense plasmas. Most people didn't know she'd done serious lab work. Some refused to believe it.

"Are you going to be leading the research on the laser?" Vee asked, as she picked up one of the blue pastries. "And do you know what these are?"

"That's crab rangoon, dyed blue to preserve some of the mystery of life," said Josh promptly. "And the research on the laser is actually what I wanted to talk to you about."

"Oh?" Vee arched her eyebrows. "Shall we get out of traffic?"

"Good idea."

Vee paused to collect a small plate of blue things and followed Josh over to one of the little round tables covered with a white cloth that always seemed to spring up like mushrooms at these gatherings.

Vee sat and pushed the pastries toward Josh, who shook his head. Vee took one and nibbled the edge. Yep, crab.

A flash of orange in the clouds caught her eyes. A delicate flurry of sparks spiraled up through the mist, tiny petals of brightness scattered through the impenetrable fog.

"Star trails." Vee smiled at the beauty of the small event. "We must be going over one of the volcanoes."

Josh checked the position readout set in the floor. "Yeah, Xochiquetzal Mons. It went active, I guess twenty years ago now."

"They're beautiful." As Vee watched, the clouds swallowed

the sparks whole, but a fresh trail swept along the wind as if these new sparks wanted to follow their friends.

Josh nodded in thoughtful agreement. "Make me nervous, though."

"Why?" Vee cocked her head at him.

A look of frank surprise crossed his face, followed by a sudden realization. "You didn't get down to the surface last time you were here, did you?"

"No need." Vee shook her head and nibbled another pastry. "I was just here for the clouds."

Josh took off his cap and smoothed his hair down before replacing it. His face said he was considering some internal question. Then, apparently, he got his answer.

"Well," he said, "you met Michael Lum, right?"

Vee nodded. In fact, she could see him through the crowd, pacing alongside Philip Bowerman talking about whatever spooks and spies talked about. Vee found herself wondering where Angela Cleary had gotten to. She did not seem to be in evidence anywhere.

"Michael's a good guy," Josh went on. "He's a v-baby. Born here. His parents were almost the first people on the station when Helen opened it up. His father, Kyle Lum, was a climatologist, and he was out doing some surveys of the lower cloud layer when the scarab ran into a star trail." He stared out at the sparks as they danced away into the clouds. "Sheered off one of the wing struts, dropped the entire scarab. They got their parachute out, fortunately, but they slammed into the side of one of the mountains. The rescue team dropped after them, within minutes, but when they got there"—Josh shook his head—"the hull had ruptured. There was nothing left."

Vee glanced back at the fading sparks. A shiver ran up her spine. "I think I'm glad I didn't know that when I was photographing them."

Josh laughed a little. "Sorry. Not the best subject of conversation, especially with a newcomer."

Vee waved his words away. "Don't worry about me. So"—she brushed a few crumbs from her skirt—"what about the laser?"

Josh took off his cap again and smoothed his hair down once more. "It's not actually about the laser," he said. "It's about getting a look at it."

"How so?"

He blew out a sigh that puffed his cheeks, put his cap back on, and looked down at his fingertips as if to see his words written there. Vee waited.

"I work on Venera on a regular basis. I do my stints here for about nine months at a time and then go home and do the lecture and paper routine. I was on Earth when the news about the Discovery dropped into the stream. When I heard about the laser, I didn't even think about it. I just got myself onto the next ship back. I assumed . . ." He shook his head and started again. "I assumed, since I was known and had a longtime affiliation with Venera, that I'd be able to get on the short list for a look at the thing, maybe even a chance to help in the analysis." He lifted his gaze. "But, no, that's not the way this is going to play. The laser is your territory for now, they're telling me. After that, maybe we'll see, but in the meantime, it's just you."

"I see," said Vee, and she really thought she did. "And you think I can get you a piece of this?"

"I don't know," he admitted. "But it seemed worth a shot."

"Why the rush?" she asked breezily. "It'll be there after I'm done with it."

The look he gave her indicated his estimation of her mental acuity had just taken a header. Vee grinned. "Got it. You want to see what the aliens left too."

"Don't get me wrong, I love my work." He tugged on his

cap's brim. "I always wanted to be out in space, but there are days when I'm very aware that I'm really just a glorified weatherman." His eyes grew distant. "This is the stuff we've forgotten to dream about."

Vee felt her grin widen. *Joshua Kenyon, you're a romantic! I thought they'd put the last of your kind into zoos.* "I don't see how there could be any problem with it. It's not as if . . ." She cut herself off but glanced around the room. There was Troy, glad-handing yet another patient Veneran with Lindi trailing behind him. There was Julia at the buffet, being photographed by Terry, and there was Robert, staring straight at her while Isaac seemed to be occupied in keeping as many bodies between him and that window as possible.

"As if?" asked Josh.

One corner of Vee's mouth turned up. "As if they've overloaded us with skilled workers. And I include myself in that." She slumped backwards and stared at her plate with its blue bits of pastry. "I swear, I don't know what they were thinking when they picked this bunch."

Josh looked at her carefully. "You really want to know?"

Vee thought about it for a minute. "Yes," she said.

Josh sighed, lifted his cap, smoothed his hair down, and replaced it. "Because you're harmless."

"What?" Vee straightened up slowly, uncertain that she'd really heard those words.

"I talked to some of the other atmosphere people about the U.N. team. I was wondering the same thing. Turns out that Grandma Helen pulled a whole set of strings to make sure whoever the U.N. sent up wouldn't be able to do much in the way of actual investigation. She wanted all the glory, and all the publications and the money, to go to Venerans."

Vee's face flushed. Anger gathered in the back of her mind. The real work to the Venerans. That she understood. But there was plenty to go around. There had to be. Wanted to get a team that couldn't do much . . . brought her up here not because they respected her skills, but because they suspected she lacked them. Just another pretty popularizer. Just another stupid face.

Vee's jaw clamped down so hard her teeth started to ache. She stood.

"Vee . . ." began Josh. "I'm sorry. I shouldn't have—"

"Don't worry about it," she said without looking at him. Her gaze swept the room until it fastened on Helen Failia, who didn't think she knew enough. Who didn't think she could do this job and had her handpicked because of that.

Vee strode across the room, barely seeing where she was going.

Slow down, Vee. Slow down! This is not going to do anyone any good, especially you. She stopped in her tracks. Her chest had tightened, and she was breathing way too hard. *Stop and think what you're doing. You throw a fit now, and you'll just be proving their point.*

In the back of her mind she heard Rosa's voice: "Be careful what you pretend to be."

Vee turned away from Failia, hoping the woman hadn't noticed her angry approach and abrupt change of plan. Evidently not. No one came up to her as she found an empty table and sat. The cameras were occupied; so were the other U.N. investigators, with each other and the cameras and with the whole wide cloudscape, and not one of them knew why they were here.

I'm gonna kill her. Vee bowed her head into one hand. *I'm gonna kill myself. What was I thinking? I actually believed—*

"Dr. Hatch?"

Vee looked up. Terry Wray stood over her.

"If this little tableau turns up in-stream—"

"It's off, it's off," Terry reassured her, lifting her hair out of the way so Vee could see the band was well and truly dark. "But are you okay?"

Vee pushed her veil back over her shoulders. "Not right now, but I will be."

"Okay, good." Terry smiled. "You're one of my star attractions. I'd hate it if you stomped off or anything."

"Oh no," replied Vee sweetly. "They're not getting rid of me that easily." A thought struck her. "Terry, can I use you shamelessly for a minute?"

A whole variety of expressions crossed Terry's face from amused curiosity to interested calculation. "As long as we stay in public, sure."

Vee squeezed her hand. "Turn that thing back on, and when I start talking to Helen Failia, come up and start paying attention, okay?"

Terry looked down her snub nose at Vee. "Okay, but I get an extra interview for this."

"Done."

Vee rose, pasted her best sunny, vapid smile on her face, and slipped over to where Helen Failia stood talking with Philip. Vee waited for a pause in the conversation and then strode forward, timing her attack.

One, two, three, she pauses for breath and . . .

"Dr. Failia, good, you're still here."

Helen turned toward Vee, all solicitous. "What can I do for you, Dr. Hatch?"

"Well"—Vee folded her hands in front of her—"I hadn't realized Dr. Kenyon was going to be on base. I thought he was still on his Earthside swing."

Helen's expression went slightly rigid as she held back some impolite emotion. "Ah, you know Dr. Kenyon?"

"By reputation. I've read his work." She glanced across at Josh and let her smile grow even happier. "I'm so glad he'll be with us. I don't mind telling you." Vee leaned forward confidentially. As she did, she saw Terry coming into range on the very edge of Helen's field of view. "I'm excited about this opportunity, but my lab work was all done a long time ago. Without someone who's in better practice, I'm afraid I might make a mess of things." She laughed lightly. Dr. Failia looked gratifyingly disconcerted.

"I'm sorry." Vee pulled back and blinked rapidly a few times. "He *is* coming down with us, isn't he? His help would be utterly invaluable to me." *Come on, there's the camera, you see it. You aren't going to admit you're sending down a half-assed team, are you?*

Helen Failia didn't even hesitate. "If you feel Dr. Kenyon can be of assistance, of course he will be included in the investigative roster." Only a slight darkness in Helen's clear eyes told Vee that she did not think this was an excellent idea.

"Marvelous." Vee beamed. "Thank you so much." For good measure, she shook Dr. Failia's hand before she turned away and strode out the door.

"That was pretty shameless," murmured Terry behind her.

"You should see me when I'm trying." Vee turned, and her smile was feral. "Thanks. Contact me when you're ready for that interview."

"Never fear." Terry's face grew thoughtful. "You should be careful about getting to like this too much, Dr. Hatch."

"You know, I've got a friend back home who says the same thing." Vee felt her face soften. "You're probably both right too."

Terry gave her one more thoughtful look. *Sizing me up,* thought Vee. *For what?* "I've got to get back," was all Terry said. "See you tomorrow."

"Bye."

Vee let her go and started walking down the corridor, suddenly both tired and frustrated. *Hope this doesn't get you in any kind of trouble, Josh, but I was not, I was* not, *going to let her get away with this. You and I.* She paused before the elevator. *We're going to make something of this, and Dr. Failia can just sit back and watch us.*

Kevin Cusmanos hated accounting. Especially late at night after an evening spent smiling and chatting with a glass of wine in his hand when what he really wanted was a beer. He hated staring at the rows of figures in their little boxes and checking them on a split screen against the individual logs where everyone was supposed to enter all their individual orders and purchases but never did.

However, it came with the job. So he sat in his office with coffee steaming in a plastic mug, ancient Afro-Country playing over the speakers, and a burgeoning dislike of Shelby Kray, one of the new guys who could not seem to get the hang of keeping track of his money.

The door, which Kevin never locked, swished open. Kevin glanced up briefly and saw Derek framed in the threshold.

"Hey," said Derek, a little tentatively. He still had his party clothes on—black slacks, red tunic, and cap.

Now's not a great time, little brother, thought Kevin, but all he said was, "Hey."

Derek wandered in and dropped down on the stiff sofa Kevin kept for visitors. Most offices had chairs, but Kevin insisted that it was traditional for a mechanic to have a rundown sofa, so a sofa he would have.

"So, when they dropping you down?" asked Derek.

Kevin eyed him, trying to see what he had really come in for. "Couple of days. Gotta get at least some training into the tourists first."

Derek tapped the back of the sofa, sort of in time with the music. "They're going to be sending Josh Kenyon down with you. Did you know that?"

"Yes." Derek still wouldn't look at him. "Ben let me know

at the end of the reception. Said it was Dr. Hatch's idea." *Come on, Derek, say it, whatever it is. It's just you and me here.*

But Derek just changed the subject again. "And you're taking Adrian with you?"

Kevin sighed and looked back down at his screen. "Yeah, Adrian will be with me in Scarab Five. Charlotte and Bailey are taking down Fourteen." The problem, he decided was that Shelby wasn't used to the idea of human backup for computer records. He'd come from a fully automated and fully profit-making environment.

Just have to take him aside and teach him the importance of counting those beans. . . .

"I don't envy you, Kevin."

"I don't envy me either," muttered Kevin before he realized Derek was not talking about correcting Shelby's accounting behaviors.

"You expecting problems?" Derek was working hard to make the question sound like idle curiosity, and he was failing miserably.

At least now I know what you wanted to talk about. Kevin leaned back with a sigh. "Actually, Derek, I am, and you should be too."

Derek shook his head and dropped his gaze, smiling a little. It was an old gesture, a little-boy gesture Derek had picked up when trying to put one over on teachers, and principals, and pretty girls. "Well, we'll just all have to do our best, won't we?" he said brightly. When he looked up again, all he saw was Kevin's blank expression.

"I guess so," Kevin ran one finger along the edge of the desk. "Dr. Meyer talk to you lately?"

Derek nodded, relaxed. "Yeah. She doesn't mind the pause. She's got lots of new data to correlate, she says, especially with the biologist they sent up."

Kevin met his brother's eyes. He saw all the uneasy trust in them, all the shaky confidence that everything was still going to be okay because not only was one of the big shots in on this, his big brother was too. A thousand things jumped into Kevin's mind all at once, all of them needing to be said. Hell, begging to be said.

Derek slapped his hands down on his thighs and got to his feet.

"Derek . . ." started Kevin.

"What?"

And if I say anything, then what? He won't stop. I'll just scare him, and if he's scared, he'll give it all away. It's not just Michael we're dealing with now. We've got the U.N. here. "Never mind."

Derek shrugged. "Okay, then. I won't."

"Okay."

Derek walked back out into the main hangar. The door swished shut behind him. Kevin rested his elbows on his desk and stared at the screen. The rows of dollar figures and time signatures made no sense. They were just numbers, tidy sets of numbers that didn't mean anything at all.

What had ever convinced him that they did?

"We were ready to make the recording, Ms. Cleary," called Phil through the open door.

"Thank you, Mr. Bowerman," Angela shouted back. "I'll be right there."

Philip and Angela had requested adjoining suites on the grounds that they'd have to be doing a lot of screen work together and they didn't want to have to monopolize a conference room. Angela wasn't entirely sure Dr. Failia believed them, but she wasn't sure she cared either.

Angela pulled out a chair from under Phil's dining table and swiveled it to face the wall screen. She sat down and flattened her screen roll on her lap. As she did, Phil pressed the Record key and started talking to the wall screen.

"Good evening, Mr. Hourani. This is preliminary report you asked for. We've had several conversations with Michael Lum, the chief of security here. He's cooperative, if not terribly enthusiastic. We've established a monitoring approach on com traffic to and from Mars that everybody can live with. . . ."

"We're monitoring transmission levels, just for the past six months as opposed to the previous couple of years, seeing if we get any jumps," put in Angela.

"We've also checked dips into known stream hot spots," Philip went on, ticking off a point on the screen roll he had spread out on his lap. "There's a few Venerans who like to talk separatist politics, but they're all in the shallows, nothing going on down in the depths." He glanced at Angela. *Your turn,* he mouthed.

Angela found her next point on her own roll. "Bennet Godwin was late to the U.N. reception tonight, but we got in a face-to-face. My impression is that he seems more sour than serious. If he's doing anything other than being sympathetic to the Bradburyans and being annoyed at U.N. interference with his schedule pad, he's doing a tremendous job of hiding it."

"In short, sir," said Philip, "so far so good. There seems to be nothing going on here but science and general good clean living." He reached for the Send key, but Angela frowned, and he hesitated.

"The only thing is . . ." She started and then stopped. Could be nothing, probably was nothing, but if it wasn't . . ." *Say it Angela.* "The tension around here is thicker than the cloud cover. During the reception, I felt as if I was in a shark pool, and the sharks were all waiting for the first hint of blood."

The corner of Philip's mouth quirked up. "You ever dealt with a research facility that's short on funding before?"

Angela shook her head. "But this one isn't anymore."

"True, but if you've been living in fear for a while, it can take time to bleed away."

Angela shrugged. "I offer it for what it's worth." She paused. "Mr. Hourani, you should also know that I will be the one going down to take a look at the Discovery with the rest of the investigative team. Phil required me to engage in an obscure North American combat ritual known as scissors-paper-stone to determine which of us would take the plunge, and I lost."

Phil's smile was all benevolence. "And on that note . . ." Philip touched the Send button, and the record light faded out in time with the glow of the screen.

Angela dropped the screen roll on the couch and yawned hugely. "Want something caffeinated?" asked Philip.

She shook her head. "I was on coffee all through dinner; any more and you'll be peeling me off the ceiling."

"Scotch then? The base distillery's surprisingly good."

She waved him away. "Want the boss to catch me with a glass in my hand? We're on the clock until he takes us off it."

"Relax, Angie, he can't see you from Earth."

"He'd smell it on the ether." Philip opened his mouth, and she held up her hand. Philip shrugged and let it go, picking up his notes instead. They each settled down to their own work and their own thoughts until the screen chimed again and lit up with an incoming message.

Mr. Hourani's head and shoulders appeared on the screen. The wall behind him was completely blank, so he was probably in his own office rather than one of the conference rooms.

"Good evening, Mr. Bowerman, Ms. Cleary," said Mr. Hourani. They'd both given him permission to use their first names, but Angela had never heard him do it. "Thank you for your initial report. Your compromise on the Venus-Mars communication monitoring is excellent. I doubt we'll see anything there, but if we do, it would be best if the Venerans see it too. We are conducting this one in the full blaze of media jurisprudence. You in particular are being watched. If we make an accusation we must be very, very certain of our facts or we will be vilified from one end of the stream to the other." He gave them a small, ironic smile. "I know. Someone is going to do that anyway, but I'd prefer it if they were wrong and we were right." Mr. Hourani turned over a sheet in front of him. "Now, as to Ms. Cleary being the one to actually visit the Discovery, all I have to say is, given Mr. Bowerman's fondness for ancient combat rituals, I would have expected you to be ready for this eventuality." He flashed a look full of his best mock severity. "I can only hope you will do better next time." His face softened instantly back into his normal, neutral expression. "Continue with your good work. I will be very interested in what you uncover." The connection faded to black.

"Excellent job, Ms. Cleary," said Phil.

"Excellent job, Mr. Bowerman," replied Angela. They shook hands vigorously. Angela rolled her screen back up and stood. "I've got training tomorrow morning. You want to get together afterwards and do an initial rundown on the Mars monitoring?"

"Sounds good." Phil stretched his arms up over his head and let them swing back down. "Tough going on the EVA stuff?"

Now it was Angela's turn to shrug. "Getting in and out of the suits is a pain, but other than that . . ." She shrugged again. "Actually, I'm kind of looking forward to this. It's not a chance that comes around every day."

"You're right there. I just"—Phil waved his hands as if

looking to catch hold of the right words—"cannot get excited about going down into that hellhole."

Angela chuckled and slapped him gently on the shoulder. "Wimp. You go through space just fine."

"Ah"—Phil held up one finger—"but if the ship springs a leak in space, chances are you'll have time to do something. One of those scarabs springs a leak, and you're going to pop like a balloon."

"Actually, I'll flatten and vaporize." She smiled at him. "They showed us a video. See you at breakfast?"

"You bet."

In her own room, Angela laid her screen roll on the desk. She stared at it for a moment, trying to understand what was bothering her. So far, the assignment had been a walk in the park. Everybody, everything, was as they were supposed to be, with just enough little variations and surprises to assure her that she was seeing them all accurately. The underlying tension could easily exist because Venera Base was a colony, a unique colony in a unique situation to be sure, but a colony all the same; and colonists did not generally like yewners, with good reason.

From the outside, Venera looked simple, but when you got inside, you saw it was anything but. It was called a research base, so everyone saw the scientists and the engineers and seldom got beyond that. But the majority of the ten thousand people on the base were not scientists. They were maintenance staff, shopkeepers, teachers, administrators, farmers, skilled and unskilled workers, children, and what Angie called "support spouses," people who kept the house and raised the children and did the business of living so the other spouse could take care of the other kinds of business. As on any isolated base, people were largely defined by what work they did. Your work determined who you socialized with, where you lived, how you were treated in the social hierarchy—and there was definitely a hierarchy, with the scientists at the top. She hadn't quite defined the bottom yet. It was somewhere between the butchers and the farmers.

Not that there were bad neighborhoods here or anything like that. Grandma Helen would never have permitted it. Everything was clean, everyone was looked after one way or another. Everyone had some kind of community to keep them going—villages within the village.

All of which helped explain one of the other things Angie had found. Some people had spent their life savings and a whole lot of time trying to get here. It was far more peaceful than Mars and, unlike the Moon, was uncontrolled by corporate interests. It was also far friendlier than Earth. There were people who saw this as paradise, and Grandma Helen as Mother Creation.

All day Angela had talked to people: on the mall, on the education level, in the food-processing plants, and all day she had heard the same thing. "Grandma Helen, she's a great woman." "Grandma Helen, she keeps this place going." "Grandma Helen knows what she's doing." It was amazing. It was a little frightening.

But still, there was something. Snippets. Near misses. Hesitations. She shook her head. She'd tell Phil about it at breakfast tomorrow. One of the things she liked about her partner and her boss was that they paid attention to unformed concerns. Maybe together Phil and she could dig out whatever her subconscious was trying to tell her.

Angela smiled. One thing was for sure. If Venera Base had secrets, it would not be keeping them for very much longer.

CHAPTER SIX

"My fellow Ca'aed continues to enjoy its health?"

The sad envy in the city's question shivered through T'sha and made her shift her weight on the kite's perches. Disease and too many sterile winds had crippled the city of K'est. Pity surged through T'sha as her kite carried her through the city's body. The supporting bones shone white around her, as bleached as the corals. The only colors seemed to be the painted shells, with their sayings and teachings written in beautiful calligraphy overlaying graduated shades of rose and lavender.

"Ca'aed has been fortunate," T'sha replied to the city through her headset. "I have brought Ambassador Z'eth a new cloning of skin cells that have worked well for us."

"Ah," sighed K'est, "I look forward to receiving them."

Although long illness had given K'est a slight tendency toward self-pity, the city was not yet dying. Far from it. Everywhere, T'sha passed people alive with purpose. They tended and studied. They sampled and directed. In several places, she saw clusters of constructors and their attendants grafting living tendons onto dead bones and transplanting coral buds that glowed pink and orange with vibrant life. Although the winds swirling outside the city were thin, inside its sphere they were thick with life and nutrition. It was almost as if the engineers had turned the entire city into a refresher chamber. T'sha felt her skin expand to take in the richness flowing all around her.

All of this life was the result of Ambassador Z'eth's tireless efforts. Another ambassador would have given up long ago and indentured her people to other cities for the best terms she could get. Perhaps she would have gone so far as to try to grow a village from what little still lived of her city.

Z'eth, however, soared over her tragedies. It was known that K'est had suggested that her people disband and allow her to die, but Z'eth would not hear of it. Instead, she had bargained and bartered for her city's needs with a zeal that left the most senior of the High Law Meet in awe. Her city, her people, were not rich and might not ever be again, but they were alive, and if they were not strong, they were still proud.

T'sha had to admit Z'eth's call for a private meeting made her nervous. Z'eth could wring promises from the clouds and the canopy, and T'sha was beholden to her on several levels. What did Z'eth want from T'sha? Or, even more important, what did she want from Ca'aed?

Z'eth's embassy lay beneath the city's central temple. The embassy was a chamber of shell and bone twined with ligaments and synaptic lace to connect it directly to the major sensory nodes of the city. What the city felt was transmitted to the embassy without the city even having to speak. Z'eth could tell by the tone and texture of her embassy walls how her city fared.

T'sha gave her kite to one of the embassy's few healthy mooring clamps and presented herself to the portal. It recognized her image and essence and opened for her.

"I have told the ambassador you are here," said K'est. "She is in the debating chamber."

"Thank you." T'sha slipped cautiously forward.

The embassy was crowded. So many people rested on the perches and floated in the air that T'sha could barely find room to glide through the corridors. T'sha glimpsed tattoos as she wove her way between them. Some were engineers and teachers, which she had expected, but most were archivists and trackers.

Of course, not even the city could keep track of all Z'eth's promises. If there is enough of the city to work complex issues . . . T'sha winced at her own thoughts. K'est lived. It would grow strong again. Z'eth was dedicated and would see it happen.

T'sha laughed softly at herself. Old superstitions. Send a bad thought out on the wind, and it would land where it began. A pessimistic thought about K'est's health could affect Ca'aed's.

At last, T'sha made her awkward way to the embassy's debating chamber. The room filled with the scent and taste of people. Words crowded the air and bumped against T'sha's wings. In the center of it all hung Z'eth, her posthands clutching a synaptic bundle as she listened to an engineer, a teacher, and an archivist. For a moment, T'sha thought she might be taking the pulse of her city as it listened to the same discussion and weighed the words.

T'sha waited politely in the threshold. Eventually, Z'eth disengaged herself from her advisers and glided a winding but still dignified path to the door.

"Good luck, Ambassador T'sha." Z'eth raised her forehands. "I'm sorry you find such a crush here. We've had a heavy day. K'est is suffering from a vascular cancer in the upper eastern districts. As you can imagine, we must work quickly."

The news shook T'sha's bones. "Good luck, Ambassador," she said hurriedly, even as she touched Z'eth's hands. "Please, allow me to return some other time. You have too much to do here without—"

Z'eth fanned her words away. "You leave for New Home in two dodec-hours, do you not?"

"Yes," admitted T'sha, "but—"

"Then my words must touch you now." Z'eth lifted her muzzle, as if tasting the air to find a quiet space. "Let us go to the refresher. It is not the place for polite conversation, but—"

"Gladly, Ambassador," T'sha dipped her muzzle.

"Then follow me, if there is room," Z'eth added ruefully.

They made their way through the corridor, sometimes flying, sometimes picking their way from perch to perch, but at last the refresher opened for them. T'sha allowed the thick air to surround her. The circulation pushed her gently from point to point, allowing her own toxins to disperse while her skin took in what nutrients the room had to offer. The walls sprouted fresh fruits and other dainties, but T'sha did not sample any, even though nervousness had emptied her stomachs.

Z'eth let the room float her for a while. It seemed to T'sha her skin was drinking deeply of quiet as well as nutrition. As T'sha watched, Z'eth swelled, opening her pores and relaxing her bones.

The moment, however, did not last. Z'eth returned to her normal size, angling her wings and spreading her crest to hold herself still against the room's circulating breezes.

"I have been following up the records of your votes, Ambassador," she said as T'sha brought herself to a proper distance for conversation. "You have been lavish with Ca'aed's promises."

T'sha resolved not to drop her gaze or twiddle her postfingers. "Now is not a good time to narrow our chances of success on the candidate world." She could not yet bring herself to call it New Home. D'seun's words still echoed through the High Law Meet. His friends were many, and they had promises they could call in at a moment's notice. Without constant countering, there was still the danger that a vote might be taken to ignore the New People altogether and simply start full-scale conversion of the candidate world into New Home.

"Ambassador T'sha," sighed Z'eth, "as one who has represented her city for a long time, let me warn you—if Ca'aed got sick now, you would have nothing to save it with."

T'sha lost her balance for a moment and drifted away. Z'eth's words touched her secret fear. She had not even voiced the worry to Ca'aed itself, although she suspected Ca'aed knew. "Ca'aed is strong and has the wisdom of years."

"The past did not help Gaith. We are flying into the nightside, Ambassador T'sha, and we may not come out." Z'eth dipped her muzzle. "Especially if we do not have New Home."

"Ambassador." T'sha hesitated. "Did I have your vote only because of my promises?"

Z'eth swelled. "No." The word was strong against T'sha's skin. "I believe you are correct. We must understand the New People. We must know they have no claim on the candidate world. If a feud began, we could be divided if there were . . . questions about our right to do as we do. We cannot be divided."

T'sha felt as if all the air had rushed away from her wings and that she must fall. "A feud with the New People? How can it even be contemplated?"

"If we both want the same thing, and we both have justifiable claims, how can it not be contemplated?" returned Z'eth. "Ambassador, I know that your mother favored teachers from the temples for your education, but you are not that naïve. We have a severe problem. We need New Home. We have New Home underneath us. We must be ready to secure it. We cannot question that."

Even if the New People truly have a legitimate claim? Ambassador, what are you asking of me? In the next moment T'sha knew, and the realization tightened her skin and bones. Z'eth wanted T'sha to go in and study the situation, as mandated by the vote in the High Law Meet. Then, no matter what she found, Z'eth wanted T'sha to say that the New People had no legitimate claim to the candidate world.

"Ambassador Z'eth . . . I cannot promise to give you the answers you want."

"I know that." Z'eth drifted even closer. The taste and touch of her words flooded T'sha's senses. "I am not asking you to say anything you do not see. I am asking you to understand how serious this matter is. How deeply we need this done. I am asking you to imagine scars on Ca'aed's hearts and the ancient walls crumbling to dust on the wind because the life has been bleached out of them. I am asking you to imagine your city in pain." She paused. "I am asking you to imagine what I have been through with K'est."

Shame and confusion shriveled T'sha. Already Ca'aed was afraid, a fact that never left her, even though her city had never spoken to her of it but that once. What if . . . ?

"I have never underestimated the dangers," said T'sha, uncertain whether she was trying to reassure Z'eth or herself.

"I think you have, Ambassador," said Z'eth, cutting her off. "I am sorry, but I believe what I say to be the truth. You are young, you are rich, and you have all the Teachings behind you. I have only my crippled city and my people promised down to their grandchildren."

T'sha clamped her muzzle shut. If she tried to speak now, she would only spurt and sputter like a nervous child. Even so, she could not believe what filled the air between them. Ambassador Z'eth wanted her to discover that the New People had no legitimate claim to the candidate world so that if those New People wished to begin a feud over the world, the

People themselves would not even consider that the New People's cause might be legitimate.

Z'eth asked for this without facts, without sight or taste or any other concrete knowledge.

She asked T'sha to tell this heinous lie because she, Z'eth, feared for her city.

No, no, that's not all, T'sha tried to banish the thought. *There is more to it than that. She fears for her city's people, for all of us.*

But even if Z'eth only feared for her city, surely that was fear enough. T'sha tried to imagine Ca'aed as ill as K'est. What would she do? What would she not do?

And she owed Z'eth heavily for her support. Without her, T'sha would not be going to the candidate world at all.

But what was the point of T'sha going to question D'seun's work if she took the answers with her?

T'sha tensed her bones. "I will remember the touch of your words," she said. "I feel them keenly. They will not fall away from me in the winds of the candidate world."

"Thank you, Ambassador," said Z'eth gravely. "That is all the promise I ask."

Thank you, Ambassador, for that is all the promise I can give. "Is there anything else we must discuss? As you said, I must leave soon, and I still have so much to settle with Ca'aed and its caretakers."

Z'eth dipped her muzzle. "Care for your city, Ambassador. May it stay strong for your return."

They wished each other luck and parted, Z'eth to find her advisers, and T'sha to find her kite.

What T'sha could not find again was her calm. As her kite flew her home, T'sha turned Z'eth's words over and over again, searching for comfort, or at least a kinder interpretation in them.

A feud with the New People. It was not something she had

even considered. If the New People had any kind of claim on the candidate world, surely, the People themselves would simply leave. Life served life. Life spread life. Sane and balanced life did not spend itself in useless contest. It found its own niche and filled it to the fullest. The People were sane and balanced and would not feud with the New People.

But what if the New People feud with us?

All of T'sha's bones contracted abruptly at the thought. *No.* She shook herself. *It could not happen. There are things which must be true for all sane life. If they have no claim, they cannot contest our claim. There would be no reason for them to. Z'eth is a great ambassador, but perhaps she has been fighting too long for the life of her city.*

Not that she is growing insane, T'sha added to herself hastily. *But perhaps her focus has narrowed.*

That was a good enough thought that T'sha could pretend to be content with it. But even so, Z'eth's words about a sudden illness touching Ca'aed left a nagging fear. Almost instinctively, T'sha ordered her headset to call Ca'aed.

"Good luck, Ambassador," came the city's voice. "How went your meeting with Ambassador Z'eth?"

T'sha deflated. "I will tell you, Ca'aed. I don't know which upset me more, Z'eth or her city."

Ca'aed murmured sympathetically. "Visiting the sick can be distressing."

A silence stretched out between them, while T'sha worked up the courage to ask the question that would not leave her alone. "Ca'aed?"

"Yes, T'sha?"

T'sha deflated even further, as if the weight of her thoughts pressed down on her. "You said . . . you said you were afraid that you would suffer, as Gaith suffered—"

"I am afraid, T'sha. I cannot help it."

"But I may find that the New People have a legitimate claim on the candidate world. What then?"

Ca'aed was silent for a long moment. When it did speak, the words came slowly, as if the city had to drag them out one at a time. "If they live in the world, if they spread life and help life, and still their life and ours cannot live together sanely, I believe we must then find another world."

Love welled up out of T'sha's soul. She did not question her city's words. If the words were not completely true, she did not want to know. She wanted only to believe. While she had Ca'aed with her, she could do anything and needed no other ally.

As Ca'aed's sphere came into view, their talk turned to the provisions made for T'sha's absence. Together they reviewed the promises of authority and caretaking and agreed to their wording. Ca'aed reported it was getting on well with Ta'teth, the newly selected deputy ambassador, but that Ta'teth's sudden elevation still made him nervous.

T'sha couldn't blame him. She knew what it was to sit cloistered in a waiting room while all the Kan Ca'aed considered your skills, your family, the promises you had made and accepted, and told the pollers who went from compound to compound whether they believed you were worthy of their trust. And this was before the question was even officially put to Ca'aed itself.

"He will calm down soon, I believe," said Ca'aed. "Wait. Ah. Your parents speak to me and ask me to remind you that you agreed to stop by your home and talk about marriage promises."

"Do they?" T'sha clacked her teeth hard, once.

"You should have your own household."

Indignation swelled T'sha back up to her normal size. "Are those your words or theirs?"

"Both."

I am surrounded. "You are my city, not my marriage broker."

"You are my citizen as well as my ambassador. I speak for your welfare. Does your own body not speak to you of children?"

"Frequently." *This is a lovely conversation to be having right now. It is not a distraction I need.*

"Well then?"

"All right, all right." T'sha rattled her wings. "Take me there. Public affairs must wait for affairs of the home and egg, it would seem."

"Sometimes, T'sha." A rare flash of humor brightened Ca'aed's voice. "Sometimes."

Ca'aed spoke to T'sha's kite and took control, guiding it between the swarm of traffic—kite, wing, and dirigible that always buzzed about Ca'aed and its wake villages. T'sha's birth family lived near the top of the city. When she was young, she and her siblings had played chase, darting in and out of the light portals that made up their personal ceiling.

The family Br'ei had encouraged a garden around the tendons that tied their private chambers to the main body of the city. Anemones in all the colors of life puffed out eggs and pollen that sparkled brightly in the approaching twilight. T'sha paused in front of the main door, intending to take time to organize her thoughts, but she misjudged her distance. The door caught a taste of her and opened.

Her birth parents waited for her in the center of the greeting room—pale Mother Pa'and who seemed to fill any room with her presence even when she was contracted down to the size of a child, and brightly shining Father Ta'ved, who had an aura of calm around him that could work on T'sha better than ten hours in a refresher. The interlocking rings of their marriage tattoos still appeared as dark and strong against their skin as they had when T'sha was a child.

Father Ta'ved's city had fallen to a slow rot, one of the first. Mother Pa'and's family could not bear the idea of their friends all falling into an ordinary term of indenture, so they arranged for Ta'ved to enter into a childbearing marriage with their oldest daughter. After two children, Ta'ved and Pa'and decided they both liked the arrangement. Ta'ved liked not having the pressures of his own house to worry over, and Pa'and found him an excellent father and friend. So, they renewed the promise. Pa'and even gave Ta'ved the option of bringing other spouses into the household, but he had never used it.

"Good luck, Mother Pa'and, Father Ta'ved." T'sha rubbed her parents' muzzles. She noticed, gratefully, that they had decided to leave her little sisters T'kel and Pa'daid out of this family conversation. T'deu had probably absented himself.

"Now." T'sha backed just far enough away so she could see their eyes. "Let me see if I can guess how this will go. Mother Pa'and, you will wish me the best of luck on my new mission." Mother dipped her muzzle in acknowledgment. Father clacked his teeth, just a little. "And you, Father Ta'ved, will mention that this is likely to be the work of a lifetime. Mother, you will agree with him and say how hard it is to do the work of a lifetime with no family to support you, to have to promise constantly and barter for everything that you need instead of being surrounded by those who are dedicated to helping you because their future and contentment are tied to yours." T'sha swelled, spreading her wings to encompass the whole room. "Father will agree profoundly, and I, so moved by your arguments, will fly instantly to the marriage broker, pick myself out three husbands and a wife, and not leave for the candidate world until my entire load of eggs is thoroughly fertilized." She subsided.

"Am I right?"

Mother clacked her teeth loud and hard, shaking with her

amusement. "You could have gone straight to the marriage broker, Daughter T'sha, and saved your breath to choose your spouses."

T'sha deflated to her normal size. "Mother, Father." She thrust her muzzle toward them, pleading. "I promise, when my business on the candidate world is done, I will graft myself onto the marriage broker until I have found someone to be madly in love with, someone to sire my children, and someone to keep my home. Will that satisfy you?"

"Deeply," said Mother Pa'and. "You will never be in a better position to make those promises than you are now."

T'sha's crest ruffled. "And if we're done predicting my imminent political death?"

"Daughter T'sha." Father Ta'ved sank just a little. "You know that is not what we're doing here."

"I know, Father Ta'ved, I know." T'sha brushed her muzzle against his. "But I have been given so much, both in responsibility and authority, that to spend time seeking after a household of my own before I've done my duty by the People and my city . . . It feels greedy."

Father Ta'ved swelled proudly. "Such a feeling does you great credit, Daughter T'sha. But children for your family and your city is not a greedy wish."

T'sha clacked her teeth, both in mirth and utter exasperation. "Enough! Mother, Father, you have my promises and I have an important appointment. Can we wish each other luck with full souls and leave all this for when I return?"

Mother Pa'and rubbed T'sha's muzzle with her own. "Of course, Daughter. Good luck in all you do."

"Stand by your feelings, Daughter," Father Ta'ved murmured as he caressed her. "They are sound and alive."

"Thank you, and good luck to you both." T'sha drifted away toward the portal. "And if, when I return, you have word of someone from a good family who is interested in perhaps two years of mutual promise to help us both learn how to set up a house and work within a marriage, I will not be sorry to hear of them."

Her parents' approval all but radiated off her back as T'sha flew out the door.

The remainder of her time passed quietly. She met with her newly selected deputy and found him much as Ca'aed described. The district speakers were content with his credentials and competence. He would do well as soon as he had something to do. She checked in with the indentures working on Gaith and found all there going smoothly, if slowly, and the quarantines being rigorously maintained.

Back at home, she played with her sisters and chatted about innocuous things with her brother and his father, pretending nothing much was happening in any of their lives.

Finally, she soaked herself long and thoroughly in the refresher, eating until her stomach groaned and her headset reminded her it was time to leave for the World Portals.

T'sha loaded herself and her tiny caretaker bundle aboard her kite. It felt her weight and let Ca'aed guide it out into the open air.

"Good luck, Ambassador," said Ca'aed as its portal closed. "I will miss you."

Sorrow deflated T'sha, although she struggled against it. In the past few hours, she had been able to forget about Z'eth's words and about D'seun's formidable support. Now, it all flooded back. "I'll be back soon, Ca'aed, with only good news."

"I believe you, T'sha," said her city. "I believe in you."

T'sha let those last words warm her all the way to the World Portals.

The portals themselves were not alive. Too much metal was required in their construction to allow them life and awareness such as the cities possessed. Instead, the great cagelike complex was maintained by a veneer of life—scuttling, twiglike constructors, flat stately securitors, and busy recorders that were all eye and wing.

T'sha reached the gate and was touched briefly by the welcomers, which identified her and opened the portals. T'sha sent her kite back to Ca'aed and hesitated, looking through at the tools swarming over the lifeless struts and conduits. She shivered. At the best of times, T'sha did not like the World Portals. They made her uneasy, gliding through a huge cage that was insensible to her presence, unable to care who she was or what she needed.

"Ambassador T'sha?" A recorder swooped into her line of sight. "Technician Pe'sen has asked this one to direct you to your portal."

"Proceed."

T'sha followed the recorder along the approved path, staying well away from the engineers, technicians, and their tools. All around her, she heard the low, strange hum of mindless machinery. The air tasted of metal and electricity. Two of T'sha's stomachs turned over, and she wished she had eaten more lightly.

The cage opened before her, and T'sha saw the seventh portal stretching out parallel with the canopy. It was a ragged starburst, like a huge silver neuron. T'sha picked Pe'sen out from among his colleagues circling the big, blocky monitor station.

"Technician Pe'sen." T'sha flew past the recorder and touched her friend's hands. "Good luck. I promise my passage will not damage any of your children." Pe'sen would go on at length about the difficulty of growing and training cortices that could adequately translate the condition of a nonliving entity.

"That's what you say now." He shook his head mournfully.

"But I know you ambassadors. If it can't vote, you don't care for it."

T'sha whistled with mock despair. "I repent, I repent. I have learned better." Pe'sen clacked his teeth at her. "Are you ready for me, my friend?"

"Always, Ambassador." Pe'sen glided back diffidently, leaving her path clear. "If you'll enter the ring, we will send you to New Home."

T'sha tried to keep her posthands from clutching her bundle, even as she tried to keep her bones relaxed. She was partially successful. She flew across the vast, open expanse of the ring until she reached the center. She hovered there, waiting, while Pe'sen and his colleagues worked their magic.

T'sha didn't understand how the World Portals worked. Pe'sen's patient explanations of the function of waves and particles, actions at a distance, and the flux-fold model of nonliving spaces brushed past her skin and left no impression. In the end, all she really knew was that Pe'sen understood it and had made it work flawlessly hundreds of times.

Then why am I ready to bolt from fear?

Through her headset, she heard Pe'sen give the activation command. The ring sang, a high, keening note. The metalic-electric taste of the air grew overwhelming. The air below her rippled with pure white light. T'sha clutched her bundle and drew tightly in on herself. The air around her bent, brightened, and pulled her down. . . . And then she was not falling down into brightness but rising up from darkness. Clear air supported her wings, and T'sha could breathe again and look around herself.

All she saw was desert. The candidate world was gold and gray in its twilight. The wind felt firm and familiar under her wings. It was strong with the scent of acid, gritty with dust, and dense with the swirling clouds and smoke from the living mountains. For all that, the wind was sterile. She could smell no life anywhere.

The sterility, though, was not distressing, as it was on Home. Here, the wind felt clean. They could do anything here, plant anything, breed anything, spread all the life they needed. New Home, new life, new hope. Her bones quivered with an excitement that was the last thing she expected to feel.

"Amazing, isn't it?" D'seun flew from his perch on the edge of the ring and hovered next to her.

"Yes," she answered, all animosity lost in wonder. T'sha tilted her wings to rise higher. Below all the winds spread a naked crust laced with cracks and ravines and double-walled ring valleys. Twilight dulled its colors underneath her. But ahead, she could see the deepening darkness of the nightside, and there, the crust glowed more brightly than she had ever seen on Home. "It truly is amazing."

She banked back to D'seun. He was speaking to the mooring cortex next to the clamp that held the portal's kite. He turned his muzzle toward her. "I am getting a signal from the base. They are not far and are moving slower than windspeed. Shall we go on our own wings?"

"I'd like that." T'sha felt herself swell at the prospect of traveling through the fresh winds.

"Let us, then." D'seun launched himself onto the wind, sailing toward the nightside with its blackened air and brightly shining crust. The twilight they flew through turned the wind a smoky gray.

"When I first came here, I never thought to find anything without life beautiful," said D'seun. T'sha started at the brush of his words. "I keep dreaming that because this world in itself is so beautiful, so balanced, the life we spread will be the same."

A fine sentiment, one T'sha could easily agree with. The wonder of the place seeped through her skin and settled into her bones, carried by the willing wind. But she could not afford to let the feelings sink so deep that she stopped thinking. That was something D'seun might be counting on.

"The balance will depend on us," she said.

D'seun said nothing in reply. They coasted together in silence. T'sha tried not to believe that D'seun was plotting strategies in his own mind, but she did not have much success.

"There is our home." D'seun pointed his muzzle over his right wing. T'sha followed the angle of his flight.

The base drifted steadily through the thickening twilight, heading toward the darkness. They were almost fully into night now. The swirling clouds glowed orange and gold with reflected light, their wrinkles and grooves turning into black patches of shadow.

"Base One," D'seun spoke into his headset, "this is Ambassador D'seun, approaching with Ambassador T'sha."

"We are open for you both, Ambassadors" came a vaguely familiar voice. "Approach as you are ready."

They were now close enough that T'sha could see between the sails. The outside of the base's shells bristled with antennae and sensors. Their roots and ligaments created a net around ten or twelve bubble chambers that reflected the crust's light even more intensely than the clouds. T'sha had stayed in similar outposts on many of her engineering journeys when she was part of the teams trying to repair the canopy.

A windward door stood open for them. T'sha and D'seun let themselves be swept inside. The door snapped promptly shut, cutting off the wind and allowing them plenty of time to slow and bank into the main work chamber.

The company inside that room also felt familiar. Researchers and engineer clung to their perches or draped across boxes of supplies and tools, watching their instruments, inscribing their reports, or talking earnestly. She had worked with such people for most of her life, before she had decided to make her opinions public.

One engineer, a dark-gold male with a deep-purple crest, climbed from perch to perch until he stood beside them.

"Welcome back, Ambassador D'seun," he said, and T'sha realized his was the familiar voice she'd heard on her headset. She scanned his tattoos quickly. "Welcome, Ambassador T'sha," he said. "I don't suppose—"

"Actually, I do, Engineer Br'sei." T'sha touched his forehands. "We worked together on the D'siash survey."

Br'sei whistled agreement. "And I'm glad to be working with you again. Let me introduce you to the rest of our team. . . ." He hesitated, his gaze sliding sideways to D'seun. "If that is acceptable, Ambassador."

"As you see fit, Engineer." D'seun settled onto a pair of perches, letting his wings furl and his body deflate.

But from Br'sei's hesitation, T'sha knew that this was not always D'seun's sentiment.

She said nothing about it. She followed in Br'sei's wake as he introduced her to the ten other members of the Seventh Team. She greeted those she knew by name and skimmed their reports. Wind acidity, speed, current direction, how the world was layered, the location of the living mountains and how frequently they erupted. Maps of seeding plans. Diagrams for new bases, equipment lists, and promises. All the concerns of a preliminary research base, but the scale was staggering.

To spread life to a whole world. To turn this desert into a vibrant garden and watch the People take possession, raise that life, and use it to spread their own life, all their lives, even further. A myriad of ideas sang inside her, swelling her up as surely as an indrawn breath.

In that moment, floating there in the still air of the analysis chamber with all the possibilities of this empty world swirling inside her, T'sha had to fight to remember there were other issues here.

"What kind of attention are we currently paying to the New People?"

D'seun looked disappointed, as if he expected the marvel of this new world to overwhelm her strange obsession with the other people. "We have mapped and timed their satellite flyovers. We arrange not to be where they are looking." A standard tactic. Stealth was important during a race to claim a resource. "If they've seen the portal, they have not made any change in routine to investigate it."

"At the moment, they are spending most of their time on one area of the crust," Br'sei volunteered. "They seem to have found something of great interest down there."

T'sha cocked her muzzle toward Br'sei. "Something they can use to spread their life?"

"We don't know . . ." said D'seun irritably, "yet."

"They are beginning to spread their machines further out across the crust," Br'sei went on, sending a disapproving ripple across D'seun's wings. "Our speculation is they are looking for more of whatever it is they've found."

T'sha gripped a perch with one of her posthands so she could keep facing Br'sei. "But have you determined whether or not they've started to make legitimate use of any resource?"

Br'sei's gaze slid uneasily over her shoulder toward D'seun. She felt the tension in the air around her and heard the small rustle of skin and bone as the other engineers shrank or swelled nervously. "They aren't mining, if that's what you mean. Unless you've determined there's another legitimate use of the crust."

T'sha's wings rippled. What had passed between Br'sei and D'seun? She felt a kind of urgency flowing from the engineer, but without words she could make no sense of it. "They might be planting. They might be building homes."

"Homes?" repeated D'seun sharply. "Don't be ridiculous. They live in the clouds."

Slowly, T'sha turned to face him where he swelled on his perches. "My point is this," she said deliberately as she pulled herself tight. "We don't know what they're doing. If it is legitimate use, we might have to change our working plan for seeding New Home."

"You could go and ask them, I suppose," said D'seun, his voice full of bland sarcasm.

"I wish that I could," said T'sha smoothly. "But the High Law Meet authorized me only to observe, and I have no doubt you will be all too happy to report me should I overfly my commission."

They eyed each other, swelling and deflating minutely in their uneasiness, very aware that they were arguing in front of subordinates in defiance of good manners and good sense. T'sha mourned for that one fleeting moment when they were joined in admiration of this new place. It had been a false promise of easier times.

Finally, D'seun settled on one size. Some of the belligerence vented from his body. "I'll be most interested to see your plan for a more thorough observation and study."

Perhaps he just hopes to keep me out of the way, thought T'sha and then she realized that was unworthy. D'seun wanted what she wanted, the birth of New Home. At the moment she was obstructing that.

She swallowed her bitter thought. "I would be willing," she said. "May I make a call for two or three volunteers?" She looked at Br'sei. He dipped his muzzle minutely in answer. He'd be willing to help.

"Certainly," said D'seun. "We will grow a chamber for you."

And perhaps this will give me a way to calm my own fears. Perhaps the New People are doing nothing legitimate. Perhaps we may take this world without taint of greed. I would like that. I would very much like that.

But the memory of the tension surrounding the engineers touched her again. No, the question was not whether something was wrong here, but what that wrong was and how far it had gone.

T'sha deflated and looked longingly at the silent walls. Already, she missed Ca'aed.

CHAPTER SEVEN

I am actually doing this. I am going to touch evidence of other life, of another world.

Raw excitement had stretched Josh Kenyon's mouth into a smile that felt like it was going to become permanent. He lay in the swaddling cradle that would serve as his crash-couch for Scarab Five's drop to the Discovery. It would also be his bed for the next two weeks. All around him, he heard soft rustles and mutters as his fellow passengers wriggled in their straps trying to get comfortable. All of them were from the U.N. team—Julia Lott, the archeologist, Terry Wray, the media rep, Troy Peachman, who called himself a "comparative culturalist" and was apparently there to look for any sociological insights and implications, and, of course, Veronica Hatch.

They were all nervous and fussy, very much a bunch of impatient tourists. But that was all right. Seeing the Discovery was worth anything—working his way up as a junior grade maintenance man, begging Vee for a slot on the team, even getting into Grandma Helen's bad books, which he had, quite thoroughly.

The morning after the reception, Dr. Failia had called him

into the Throne Room, a place he'd been to only a couple of times before. While he'd stood awkwardly in front of her desk, she'd reviewed something on its screen that seemed to absorb her whole attention. At last, he realized she wasn't going to invite him to sit down. So he sat without invitation and got ready to wait.

She kept him there in silence for another good five minutes before she finally looked up to acknowledge his presence.

"Thank you for coming, Josh," she said, with only the barest hint of politeness in her voice. "I wanted to inform you personally that Dr. Veronica Hatch of the U.N. investigative team has requested your presence to help her examine the Discovery's laser." Dr. Failia's voice was calm but tinged with something unpleasant—suspicion, maybe, or disapproval. Josh sat there with a stiff smile on his face, torn between elation and feeling like a guilty child.

"Since you'll have far more experience with EVA's than any other member of that team, I'm counting on you to take the position of team leader, to show the others around the Discovery and make sure they do minimum damage to the site."

"But, Dr. Failia . . ." Josh spread his hands. Despite the cold look she gave him, Josh forced himself to continue. "Kevin Cusmanos has a thousand times more experience than I do. Shouldn't he be going out with the team?"

"That was the initial plan." Dr. Failia's eyes grew hard. "But we want as few people down there as possible. Every new bootprint runs the risk of damaging something priceless. Since you're going, you get to baby-sit and Kevin gets to do what he is specifically trained for—supervising the scarab and the essential mechanical support system for the team."

Josh swallowed. "Yes, of course."

"Thank you, Josh," she said without warmth. "I appreciate your help."

Did she know I talked Vee into this? Or was she just peeved that one of the yewners monkeyed with her plan? Josh shook his head at the ceiling. He had no way of knowing. The whole interview had left him confused. The times he had talked with Dr. Failia before, she had been businesslike but friendly, quick with a small joke or useful observation. He'd never seen her so forbidding.

It doesn't matter. You're here. You can worry about the rest of your life later.

The low ceiling over him held a view screen that was controlled from down in the pilot's seat. Right now, it showed an image of the hangar seen through the scarab's main window and surmounted by the back of Adrian Makepeace's head and shoulders.

"Please make sure the status lights over your couches are all on the green," Adrian was saying. "We have no flight insurance. Anybody who doesn't have a green, just holler, and we'll make sure there's nothing else to holler about. Any nongreens?"

"Going once, going twice . . ." added Kevin Cusmanos.

Josh reflexively checked the four indicator lights at the bottom of his screen. All of them shone bright green, indicating he was properly strapped in.

"They're enjoying themselves, aren't they?" murmured Julia from the couch next to Vee's.

"I don't think they get many tourists out here," said Vee. Josh heard her squirm and couldn't blame her. The couches took getting used to. He also decided not to correct their impressions of what the pilots thought of them. He'd spoken out loud that once to Vee at the reception, and she still got an angry gleam in her eye when she had to talk to Grandma Helen.

"Not many tourists?" muttered Julia. "Not too many people interested in a dive into Hell? Imagine."

Josh rolled his eyes up to try to get a glimpse of the women.

He could see Veronica's feet, and Julia's. He could also see part of Julia's hand, which clutched the side of her couch so hard the fabric bunched up in her grip.

"Are you going to be all right?" asked Vee.

"Eventually, yes," Julia sighed. Josh watched her deliberately relax her hand. "This is just like being at the top of the thrill vid, you know? I hate this part."

"It gets easier," volunteered Josh. "Wait until you've done a dozen or so."

Josh spoke with more confidence than he felt. Most of his work had to do with atmospheric particle scattering, which could be done from the comforts of Venera Base and its optics lab. He could count his trips down to the surface on the fingers of one hand.

"A dozen or so," murmured Julia. "There's something to look forward to."

"It's the adventure of a lifetime," intoned Troy Peachman from his couch on Josh's right. "You should be alive to every facet of the experience."

"Alive is what I'm hoping for."

"We could record you," suggested Terry Wray helpfully. She had the couch to Julia's left. "That way you could work on your reactions each drop until you've got the keeper. Something suitably calm, yet awestruck."

"Next time," answered Julia. "I want a run-through first."

"Always a good idea," said Terry. "I can't tell you how many disasters I've had to shoot that missed all the dramatic impact just because the victims wouldn't take a minute to get their responses right."

"Well then," came Adrian's voice through the intercom, reminding them all that the speakers were open on both ends. "Let's see if we can get it right."

"Wing deployed and green at twenty percent inflation. Drop conditions green. Scarab status is go," said Kevin.

"Ready when you are, Control."

"Ready, Scarab Five," said yet another voice, this one from the hangar control. "Opening doors."

"See you on the up-trip," said Kevin.

Josh thought he heard Troy breathe something about "falling into history" but hoped he was wrong.

The view screen's feed switched down to a camera in the scarab's belly. The desk rolled past underneath them, fast and faster, until it shot away, leaving a swirl of impenetrable gray cloud.

The scarab fell. As always, Josh's stomach lurched and his body strained against the straps. His heart flipped over, a purely reflexive reaction. There was nothing he could do about it but lie there, keep his eyes on the screen, and concentrate on controlling his breathing.

On our way. They won't call us back now. We're really going to do this! The smile on his face stretched even wider.

Layers of cloud pressed against the camera. Adrian's voice, again for the sake of the tourists, droned through the intercom.

"Wing position optimized," said Adrian calmly. "Everybody okay up there? Just relax and let the couch take care of you. We're at forty-eight kilometers and looking good."

All at once, the clouds parted. Below them spread the surface of Venus, as red and wrinkled as anything Mars had to offer. It was getting closer at a rate that made Josh's heart flip over again.

"Inflating wing," rumbled Kevin. "Wing inflation at fifty percent."

Outside, the ground's approach slowed to a more leisurely pace. Features began to resolve themselves. Some wrinkles became riverbeds cut by ancient lava. Others became delicate ripples in the ground, like furrows plowed by a drunken farmer. The colors on the ground divided into rust red, burnt

orange, and sulfur yellow with streamers of coal black drifting through them.

"Beautiful," breathed Troy, and this time Josh had to agree
with him.

"Fifteen kilometers from touchdown and everything green
and go," said Adrian. "You're not getting the most interesting
landscape, but it's tough to make a good landing anywhere interesting."

"Julia, have you opened your eyes yet?" asked Veronica.

"No," Julia said, her voice pitched only slightly higher than
normal. "I'll wait until we get to the ground."

"Suit yourself." Vee shrugged in her straps. "The colors are
amazing."

"I'll bet."

"Three kilometers," said Adrian. "If you squint to the upper
right of your screens, you'll see beacon A-34, which means
we're right on target."

Beneath them, the largest furrows spread apart. Smaller
furrows following the same drunken path appeared between
them. The whole plain became a huge, wrinkled, color-
splashed bedsheet, bent at the edges, as if viewed through a
fish-eye lens. The high-pressure atmosphere played all kinds
of interesting tricks with the light.

The patch of ground Josh could see became smaller and
darker, until only a few rocks were visible. Then nothing but
blackness, followed fast by a crunching noise from below.
The scarab came to rest on a small slope, tilted up and to the
left.

"And that, ladies and gentlemen, is a perfect landing," said
Kevin. "You are now free to come out and see the world
through the big window."

Julia was already fumbling with her buckles. Vee obviously
took a second to read the directions beside her screen, because
she was on her feet and heading out into the main cabin be-

fore Julia was even sitting up. Josh waited behind to make sure Julia, Troy, and Terry had successfully extricated themselves and then followed Veronica out.

Outside the front window, the rumpled landscape stretched as far as he could see. The horizon, such as it was, was lost in a dim blur that might have been dust or mountains or simply the thick atmosphere distorting the light. They were a fair way into the long Venusian day. The dim sunlight that filtered through the clouds showed a ground that reminded Josh of the Painted Desert; red, brown, orange all mixed together along with great stretches of black, rippled stone left over from old lava flows. Here and there, an outcropping of halite or obsidian glinted dully in the ashen light.

Josh watched the investigative team crowd around the pilot seats, craning their necks to see out the window. Then he saw the muscles in Kevin's jaw tighten.

"We've got a drive ahead of us," Josh said, trying to sound polite, if not cheerful. "We can use the time to get into suits. That way there'll be less of a delay when we reach the Discovery."

And less time Kevin has to deal with you guys crammed into the cockpit.

As if to confirm Josh's thought, Kevin glanced up at him and Josh read a silent thank-you in his eyes.

The statement brought universal agreement, and the team of tourists started filing back toward the changing area. Vee gave Josh a knowing look as she passed. Yeah, she would be the one to figure out what he was really trying to do. That was all right as long as she didn't try to counteract it. Kevin gave Adrian the nod, and Adrian unbuckled himself to follow the tourists.

"And here's where the fun really starts," he muttered to Josh as he passed.

You'll forgive me if I agree with the words and not the tone, thought Josh as he followed Adrian down the corridor to the suit lockers. *I can't believe we're almost there.*

The scarab crawled forward along the uneven ground. Its bumping, rocking motion added to the confusion of the suit-up procedure, but eventually Josh and the rest of the team all got safely into their hardsuits. Adrian, with Josh's help, double-checked everyone's equipment and connections and made them run down the displays to make sure those were all functional.

Everything looked green and go. Mechanical failure in the suit—joint failure, pump failure, loss of seal integrity—any of these could mean instant death. If that knowledge added extra tension to the team, Josh couldn't see it. Even Julia, now that she was on the ground, seemed to have calmed down and become wrapped up in the business of checking her equipment, as if this were something she did every day.

Admit it. You can't see beyond your own nose right now, unless it's to look at that hole in the ground, Josh admonished himself. But he couldn't really make himself care. The Discovery waited for them. He had made it. He was going to be inside, soon, very soon.

Finally, the scarab came to a lurching halt.

"We're here!" called back Kevin.

Here. We're here. I'm here.

The U.N. investigators climbed into the airlock. Josh closed the interior hatch and found a place on one of the benches. The pressurization pump's steady chugging filled the air. Next to him, Terry Wray fussed with the camera on her chest. Her normal band rig wouldn't be able to tolerate the conditions out there, so she'd have to make do with the equipment that came with the suit, and from the look on her face, it did not meet her standards. He watched Julia Lott's lips move as she removed something on her private log channel. Next to her, Troy Peachman did the same. It looked like the two of them were holding a whispered conversation. Vee, sitting on the bench between them, flashed Josh one of her mischievous grins.

"Some fun, eh?" Her voice sounded harsher than normal through the intercom. Josh wondered if she might actually be nervous.

"Not yet," he answered. "But trust me, it will be."

Now, Josh could feel the tension winding the whole team tight. The small talk and idle speculation picked up pace, as did the meaningless shifting of weight and all the other little movements restless people make when waiting. There were the usual complaints about trying to use helmet display icons that relied on eye movement and how the water-straw kept bumping up against your chin. Finally, Troy Peachman heaved himself to his feet and started pacing between the inner hatch and the outer.

Veronica watched him for about two minutes before she apparently had enough. "Oh, sit down, Troy, it's not going anywhere."

"How do you know?" he asked with the bluff humor he apparently cultivated. "Aliens put it here. Maybe they're out there taking it away again."

Terry tried folding her arms and found that didn't work. "If they were going to do that, they would have notified me."

"You?" asked Troy, surprised.

"Yeah. I'm a media drone. We're all aliens. Didn't you know that?"

"I had wondered," replied Troy blandly.

A brief collective laugh filtered through the intercoms. Before it died, the light above the outer hatch flashed green, indicating pressurization was complete.

Instantly, everyone was on their feet. Josh worked the locking lever on the outer hatch. With a clank and a thump, the hatch swung inward to reveal the rough, intensely colored world beyond.

"Have a good trip," said Adrian as Josh stepped out. Dust and stone crunched beneath his boot. To the right loomed the cliffs of Beta Regio, with its volcano thrusting up toward the boiling sky and ribbons of lava trailing down its sides. On the edge of his vision, Josh saw Scarab Fourteen creeping down beside a fresh, flowing lava stream, and he wondered how Charlotte Murray and her crew were holding up with their load of tourists.

Then he saw the Discovery's entrance squatting in front of them, and the rest of the world went away. He took three heavy steps forward before he remembered he was supposed to be leading a team out here.

His eyes found the intercom icon and opened the general channel. "Okay, everybody, try to step where I step. The ground is pretty lumpy out there."

They only needed to cross about ten meters to the hatchway. The hardsuits and the uncertain footing made it slow going, but with every step, the hatchway got a little bigger, a little clearer. He could see the handles on the side of the lid, make out the dim reflections on the curve of its gray ceramic sides, see the little scores and pits that had been made by the burning sand brushing past on the lazy wind.

Then he was standing next to it. It was there, under his glove. He couldn't feel anything, but he could see his hand on the lid.

It was a long moment before he realized the others had ringed the hatch and stood waiting for him.

"I'll open the hatchway now." Josh grasped two of the handles, bent his knees, and shoved. The cover swung aside, just as he'd been told it would. Julia clapped her hands in silent applause. Veronica stooped and ran one gloved finger over the handle he'd just used, and grunted. Peachman tromped forward eagerly.

"Hold on," said Terry. "Can we get a shot of the empty shaft?"

"Sure." Josh stepped back and let Terry come forward and point her camera and light down the steep well with its ladder. *Just don't take too long.* He laughed silently. *Get a hold of yourself. Vee was right, it's not going anywhere.*

"Got it," Terry said, sounding satisfied. She stepped back from the hatch and turned toward him.

"Okay," said Josh, trying to keep his voice calm, as if he had already climbed down into the Discovery a hundred times. "I'll go first and show you how it's done."

Josh planted his boots onto the first rung and, moving carefully, started climbing down the well. Darkness engulfed him and his suit's lights clicked on, illuminating the black rock with its charcoal veins. He had to keep himself pressed close to the rungs to prevent his backpack from scraping against the shaft wall. His throat tightened. He'd never been inside Venus before, and he could not escape the feeling that he was being swallowed.

Josh's boot touched level stone and his lights showed him the bubble-shaped room dubbed "Chamber One." He moved back from the ladder.

A shiver ran up his spine. *This place is not ours. This is other. There is someone else out there, and we know nothing about them.* That was too huge and too strange a thought not to merit a moment of sheer wonder.

There wasn't even that much to see here—the base of the ladder, the six holes gaping beside the smooth curving wall. The real prize lay through the narrow tunnel that opened by his right hand. Down there lay Chambers Two and Three and the laser.

"Okay, next," he said into the intercom. "Keep close to the

rungs; don't bump your pack if you can help it." They'd all been briefed and run through the simulators, but it wouldn't hurt to remind them.

"Yes, Papa," said Vee. He watched her green form descending carefully, foot searching momentarily for each rung. But she reached the bottom without incident and came to stand beside him.

"Next," Josh said.

"Here we go," answered Julia. While the archeologist worked her way down, Veronica walked over to look at the inner doorway, if a small, rounded entry to a low tunnel could be called a doorway. Josh was torn between watching Vee and keeping an eye on Julia, who, if anything, was moving less steadily than Vee had, and wishing they would all *hurry up*.

"Vee, what are you doing?" asked Josh, to distract himself. She was crouched down and running her fingers over the threshold.

"Exploring the secrets of the universe," she answered. Her voice sounded flat, tight.

Troy descended right after Julia, followed closely by Terry. As soon as Terry was down, she whistled softly and began examining the smooth, rounded walls. Julia bent over the six holes laid out in a straight line at the base of the ladder. Josh was willing to bet she was talking animatedly into her log. Veronica stayed where she was, turning from the inner threshold to the mouth of the entry shaft and back again. Troy just stood in the middle of it all, a look of sheer delight on his face.

"Incredible. It just feels incredible."

Although part of Josh suspected Troy was, yet again, playing for the cameras, part of him nodded in agreement. He'd run through the videos and holographs a hundred times, but that was nothing compared to standing in the middle of the Discovery, feeling the stone surrounding them and wondering, just wondering.

Freed from his initial bout of amazement, Troy started hopping around the chamber like a kid in a candy store. He bent over the six holes with Julia; he ran his hands over the inner threshold with Veronica. He peered eagerly over Wray's shoulders to see whatever it was they were looking at, all the time murmuring, "Incredible, incredible."

"Can we see the rest?" asked Veronica abruptly.

Josh blinked. "Sure." *And I thought it was just me who couldn't wait.*

"One second," said Terry. "I need a shot of all of you with the light from the shaft coming down." She shuffled closer to the ladder. "Say cheese, but keep on doing what you're doing." People bent or walked, stiffly and reluctantly, but Josh supposed that would later be put down to the suits and the pressure. "Okay. All done."

Great. "Okay. The main chamber is through here." Josh gestured down the horizontal tunnel. "Again, I'll go first. It's hands and knees. Go slow and try not to bump your packs."

The inner tunnel was even more constricting than the entry shaft. The smooth, narrow way was completely dark except for the small black-and-gray area illuminated by his suit lights. He crawled forward without feeling anything but the insides of his gloves against his hands and the padding of his suit under his knees. There was no sound except his own breathing.

"It makes a slight rise here in the middle," he told the people behind him, whether they were following or waiting in Chamber One. He couldn't tell. There was no room for him to turn his head to look. His general plate displays told him only that their intercoms were up and running, not where those intercoms were.

The tunnel undulated sharply, forcing Josh flat onto his stomach. He shinnied up to the rounded crest and slid back down again. He hoped none of his tourists would find this too much for their dignity. Probably not. Troy seemed the most likely to make a fuss, and he wouldn't do it while there was a risk of being recorded. If they were nervous about the world around them, they seemed to be burying that feeling under the excitement of exploration.

Another two meters and the tunnel opened up into Chamber Two, the main chamber of the Discovery.

Josh got to his feet and turned around in time to see Veronica emerge from the tunnel. She stood up and moved back from the tunnel's mouth, turning as she did so she could take absolutely everything in.

Chamber Two was a bubble, like Chamber One, but three times as big and twice as high. Michael Lum had joked that this was obviously an alien church, because it was so hole-y. Circular niches a meter around and ten centimeters deep had been carved into the walls. Small shafts perforated the floor, ranging between one and six centimeters in diameter. Robot surveyors sent down those shafts found they interconnected at different levels underground. Maybe they once held a pipe network.

Tiny holes that sank into the walls at regular intervals might have been for staples or brackets of some kind, holding up shelves or wiring or clothes pegs for all they knew. An entire section of floor had been dug away for about a half meter, making a shallow, smooth-walled depression at the eastern curve of the chamber. At the bottom of the depression were still more holes—two ovals of eight holes each were surrounded by numerous minute holes drilled at seemingly random intervals.

Not even the stark evidence of human intervention could dampen Josh's delight at finally standing in the middle of the Discovery. Every last one of the holes now had a cermet tag next to it with a number designation. It had taken almost a week just to get all the holes tagged. The measurements still weren't finished. Hopefully Julia would be able to make a contribution to that effort with the miniature survey drones she carried in her pack.

From the ceiling hung three quartz globes. Inside them, you could see a tangle of filament wires. Big, pressure-tolerant, alien light bulbs. No one had managed to find the power source though, and God, how they'd looked.

A low, round doorway opened across from the tunnel. This one led to another smaller bubble room, almost a closet. Chamber Three. The laser was in there. Josh's curiosity was almost a physical force pushing him toward that other doorway. He kept still with difficulty while, one at a time, the remainder of the team emerged from the tunnel.

Every last one of them looked up and around, just as Veronica had. Josh had a feeling a number of jaws had dropped open. It even took Terry a moment before she started systematically aiming her camera again.

After that, it was a replay of the scene in the antechamber, except nine times more intense. Snatches of competing conversations jammed the radio until everyone remembered about the private channels. Troy and Julia crowded the edge of the pit, pointing and gesturing. Terry tried to record everything at once. Only Veronica didn't move. She stood in the middle of Chamber Two and frowned up at the lights.

In return, Josh frowned at her. He opened a private channel between them. "Vee? We're here to see the laser?"

She focused on him slowly, as if his words reached her from a long way away. "Yes. Right."

"This way." He pointed to the low doorway. His hand almost shook with eagerness. *Let the other tourists fend for themselves for a while. Let's see what the neighbors left for us.*

Josh ducked through the low doorway, for the moment not

really caring if Vee followed him. He turned to the right, and there it was.

The laser rig stood next to the far wall of Chamber Three. Whoever hollowed out the chamber had left behind a single wedge of polished rock. It had been planed off at a forty-five-degree angle and tapered up from the floor until it was about level with Josh's waist. A mechanism fastened to its surface and pointed toward a pair of short, narrow holes let in the ashen light from the surface.

Clumsily, Josh sat down. Now the laser rig was about level with his nose. "We're dealing with little green men all right," he said to Vee. "If this was working height for them, they couldn't be much more than a meter tall."

Vee said nothing. She just sat down beside him.

The laser itself was nothing much to look at right off. Its body was a dull-gray half-pipe about a meter long. Two tubes with roughly triangular cross sections projected out of it and pointed toward the holes to the surface, their flared ends almost touching the living rock.

"There's a set of staples down here," said Josh, leaning into the base of the half-pipe and pointing to the thick metal fasteners. "They pull out." He gripped one carefully in his thick glove fingers and pulled as gently as he could. The staple eased out a little ways, then stopped.

"Anybody analyzed the cover?" asked Vee.

"It's a ceramic. They think it's refined from local earths. Maybe shaped by some kind of laser tomography."

Vee just grunted. Josh pulled out the remaining staples. Then he lifted the cover away to reveal an interior that glittered with black glass, crystal, and gold.

And there it all was—the power points tucked into the two long, black glass (maybe) tubes, with what were unmistakably Brewster windows set into either end. The tubes themselves contained . . . what? They didn't know yet. Mirrors of incorruptible gold (probably gold. Looked like gold) stood at either end of the tubes. Golden strips had been laid down in neat patterns along the tube supports. Pairs of thick lenses had been positioned at the end of each tube that was closest to the wall, with the smaller of the pair on the inside (almost definitely a beam expander), and in front of them was a pinplate to focus the light and send it . . . where? He looked at the holes to the surface. To do what?

Much of the answer to that question would depend on what was in those black tubes, which would tell them what kind of laser they were dealing with. The presence of the tube told them it was a gas laser, but what kind of gas laser?

When they knew what kind of laser it was, they could work out what it had been used for. And when they knew what it was for, they would know what these people were doing here, and when they knew what these people were doing here . . . the universe would open up wide.

He wanted to say this to Vee, but he didn't. Something was wrong with her. She seemed closed off, and he couldn't tell why.

Well, you can sort that out later. "Can you get the monochrometer out of my pack?"

"Right." Vee stumped around behind him and he felt the small jostlings as she undid the catches on his pack and pulled out the equipment.

While Vee squatted next to the laser to position the boxy analyzer and pump down the suction cup at its base, Josh pulled their portable floodlight out of her pack and lined it up with the monochrometer on the other side of the tubes. When both devices were switched on, pure white light would shine through the tubes into the monochrometer, which would analyze the absorption patterns and report. Then they'd know what lay inside the opaque glass.

Vee jacked the monochrometer into her suit. "Okay. Go."

Josh pressed the power-on switch and the light flashed on, so suddenly and intensely bright his faceplate dimmed. He imagined a faint humming as its beams passed through the tubes. Another shiver of fear and excitement went through him, brought by the awareness that he was doing something no one else had ever done before. Even Vee's closed expression softened as she read off the monochrometer's conclusions. "Okay, we've got hydrogen in there, a little neon, and"—she paused—"carbon dioxide." She stared at the device. "It's a CO_2 laser, Josh."

"Makes sense, doesn't it?" Josh was aware he was grinning like an idiot. "Not only does CO_2 make for a versatile, powerful laser, but our aliens have been making heavy use of local materials. If there's one thing Venus has and to spare, it's CO_2."

"Right." Vee pulled the monochrometer jack out of her glove's wrist, turned her back, and left.

Josh did not let his jaw drop. Veronica marched through Chamber Two and climbed back into the tunnel toward Chamber One.

"What was that?" came Troy's voice.

I have no effing idea, thought Josh.

"Is there a problem?" Julia stood up from her crouch over the carved-out section of floor.

"No, no." Josh waved them back. Both curious and confused, he crawled back through the tunnel to Chamber One. He got there just in time to see Vee climb the last rungs of the ladder and disappear over the side of the hatchway.

Josh opened their channel. "Vee? Vee? What are you doing?"

No answer. Josh flicked over to the channel for the scarab. "Adrian? This is Josh."

"I hear you, Josh, what's up?"

"How's Dr. Hatch's suit doing?"

"She's green and go here. Something wrong?"

I have no effing idea. Josh stared at the ladder. He did not want to chase after her. If she wanted to be a temperamental artiste, that was her business. The laser was waiting for them both. If she didn't care, fine.

Except that there were so many ways she could get herself killed out there.

Josh carefully closed down all his com channels except the one to the scarab. When he was sure no one could hear him but Adrian, he started swearing softly, and he climbed the ladder back to the surface.

As he emerged from the hatch, he saw Vee crouched about ten meters away, apparently staring at one patch of ground.

"Vee? What the hell are you doing?" Josh demanded as he started stumping toward her.

"More holes." She pointed.

"Yes, I know. We found those. They should be tagged." Two squares of four small holes drilled neatly into the earth on the right side of the hole the laser pointed through.

"Yes." She stood up and started walking back toward him. Josh stopped in his tracks.

"You want to tell me what's going on?"

Apparently, she didn't. She said nothing as she passed him and climbed back down the ladder. Josh choked off another set of curses and returned to the hatch. While he watched, she lumbered down the rungs, walked to the center of the chamber, and laid down on her back, her faceplate pointing up at the ceiling.

Bewilderment warred with exasperation as Josh climbed down the ladder and stood over her. "Are you okay?"

"Fine, thank you." Her voice was bland, almost bored, and her expression matched.

"Are you going to be able to get up all right?"

"I'll call if I can't."

He paused. "You having an artistic snit of some kind?"

"Probably. You're in my way."

"Excuse me." Josh stepped back and wished he could run his hand through his hair. He just watched the still form lying on its back and staring at the ceiling, looking for all the world like an empty suit that had fallen over. *Well, so much for the idea that you'd turn out to be the reasonable one.*

Seeing nothing else to do, Josh crawled back through the tunnel to Chamber Two.

"Is Veronica all right?" asked Troy.

"She's fine," Josh assured them all as he straightened up. "She's decided to pursue an independent investigation."

Those few words satisfied everyone. *Everybody knows how artistes are,* thought Josh as he returned to Chamber Three. *I wonder how much she trades on that?*

He pushed the thought aside. Whatever Veronica wanted to do—as long as it didn't actively involve killing herself, damaging equipment, or wrecking the site—didn't really matter. He could still work. Every part of the laser had to be measured, labeled, gently sampled, and precisely cataloged and videoed. The work and the wonder of it all soon swallowed up thoughts of anything else.

Every so often, movement in Chamber Two caught his eye. Vee went back and forth between the main chamber and the antechamber three separate times. Once, she came into the laser chamber and just sat by the wall for a while. He ignored her. Eventually, she left.

At 14:00, his suit clock chimed. So, he knew, did everyone else's, but he spoke into the intercom anyway. "That's time, folks. We need to head back."

"Another few minutes—" began Troy.

"We've got two weeks," replied Josh. "You don't want to run low on coolant out here, do you?"

That got them. All at once, everyone was ready to go. No

doubt Derek had showed them the record of Deborah Pakkala, whose coolant circulation had failed on her, and how she had cooked to death in her suit before she reached the scarab, twenty meters away. Josh eyed the radio icons to flip over to the channel for Scarab Five. "Adrian, Kevin, we're coming in."

"Roger that, Josh," came back Adrian's voice. "We'll be ready for you."

Josh took a quick head count. All present, except for Vee.

"Vee?" called Josh over the public channel. "Time."

"I heard" came her voice, clear, tight, and slightly bored, as it had been for the entire afternoon.

Shaking his head yet again, Josh led the way back through the tunnel. He shinnied over the rise and stopped. Vee's suit, on its back again, blocked the tunnel.

"Vee," he said, refusing to be surprised or angry. She would not take the wonder of this day from him. He would not let her.

"Right." Using the tunnel walls as traction, she turned herself over onto her stomach and crawled out ahead of him.

Josh led the team up the ladder and across the rough, barren ground to the scarab. The airlock hatch stood open, waiting for them. They took their spots on the benches. Josh shut them inside and signaled Adrian. The outer hatch's light blinked red as the depressurization started.

"So, Dr. Hatch," began Troy conversationally. "Did you find what you were looking for?"

"Not yet." She gave him a sunny, meaningless smile. "But as Josh said, we've got two whole weeks."

"Two weeks," said Julia less enthusiastically. "If it doesn't kill us. I feel like I've been lifting weights for four solid hours."

"It's the pressure," said Troy. "We'll get used to it, I'm sure. Isn't that right, Josh?"

Josh shrugged but then remembered his suit wouldn't show the movement. "Not really, no, but you learn your limits and how to pace yourself."

"Do you think you'll ever get used to the idea you're crawling around inside an alien artifact?" asked Terry.

Josh felt his mouth quirk up. "Is this on or off the record?"

Terry sighed exasperatedly. "Civilians. If the answer's really good, I'll ask to use it."

"My God, an ethical feeder," murmured Josh, and the remark earned him a round of laughter. "The answer is, no, I don't think I'll get used to it, and I don't really want to get used to it. We are in the middle of the most incredible thing that's ever happened and I never want to forget that." He smiled. "Good enough to use?"

"Are you kidding?" said Terry. "The boss willing, I'm going to open with that."

"And what about you, Veronica?" Troy angled himself to face her. "How did you feel inside the Discovery?"

Veronica didn't move. "Oh, I was impressed," she said distantly. "Very impressed. The sheer scale of the undertaking. It's amazing."

The team nodded solemnly.

The depressurization finished, and the green light shone over the inner hatch. Josh worked the hatch and everyone spilled gratefully over into the changing room. Adrian stood ready to help them out of the bulky suits and supplied cold water from the scarab's fridge. Josh glanced down the corridor and saw movement through the main window. Team Fourteen was on the ball and heading down for their turn at the Discovery.

By the time Josh looked up from his water bottle again, Vee had vanished. The rest of the team crowded around the kitchen table, eating sandwiches and drinking water and fruit juice in quantity. They all speculated freely and at top volume about what they'd seen, what it meant, and how they were going to frame their findings for Mother Earth. Vee did not reappear.

Conscience caught up with Josh. He drained the last of his juice and climbed through the side hatch to the sleeping cabin.

Veronica sat cross-legged on her coach with her briefcase open in front of her, typing frantically. Her lips moved as the keys clacked, but he couldn't make out what she was saying to herself.

"Are you all right, Vee?"

She looked up, startled, and for a moment he saw naked anger on her face. She wiped it away. "Fine."

What is it? What is the matter with you? He sat on the edge of the floor. "You really should at least have something to drink."

She reached down next to the couch and pulled out a bottle of water. "I'm fine, really."

"Anything you want to talk about?"

Anger flickered back across her features. "No."

One more try. "You know, this is supposed to be a team effort."

"I'd heard," she replied dryly.

Leave it alone, he told himself. *Let her play her game. This is not your business.* But there was a challenge in her eyes that grated at him. No, not a challenge, an accusation.

Josh picked his way to her couch. "What have you found?" He crouched down next to her.

With three keystrokes, Veronica blanked her screen. "Nothing I'm ready to talk about."

"Listen to me," he whispered fiercely. "You've got an act going, fine. You can play with Peachman's head, and Wray's. But you play with the Discovery, and so help me, I will make such a stink you will be booted all the way back to Mother Earth without benefit of shuttle. This is not a gallery show.

This is so far beyond important we can barely understand its implications. I will *not* let you screw around with this."

Vee's angry eyes searched his face. Josh did not let his expression waver or soften. At last, Veronica dropped her gaze. Her fingers moved across the command board and typed out one line of text. She turned the screen toward him. Josh read it and his heart thudded hard in his chest.

It's a fake.

Josh sat back on his heels and met Vee's gaze. "You're out of your mind."

She frowned hard and typed.

Keep it down! We have no idea who's in on this. Go back to dinner. Tell them I overdid it and am taking a nap. Whatever. Get your briefcase out and mail me. I'll spell it out.

She added her contact code at the bottom.

Josh looked at her again. Vee's face and eyes had hardened. Whatever she'd found, or thought she'd found, she was serious about it, and if she was right. . . .

No. She can't be.

Without another word, Josh returned to the kitchen nook.

"Everything all right?" asked Troy.

"Oh yeah," lied Josh, picking up his empty juice cup and carrying it to the sonic cleaner so he wouldn't have to stay at the table and look at anybody. "It's easy to overdo it out there if you're not careful. Vee just needs to lie down and get some extra fluids."

And get her head examined. He shut the cup in the cleaner. *God, if she's doing this for self-aggrandizement, I'll kill her.*

The meal finished, the dishes got cleared, and people spread out as much as the scarab allowed, giving each other the mental space necessary for sane and civil interaction in a confined space. Adrian shuffled back to the changing area, probably to run the post-EVA suit checks and recharge batteries and tanks. Kevin was up front in the pilot's seat, running over something on the main displays. Terry commandeered one corner of the kitchen table and downloaded the day's records into her smart cam. She watched the display, apparently oblivious to anything else. Julia retreated to the couch compartment.

Josh went into the analysis nook, opened one of the overhead compartments, and retrieved his own briefcase. Perched on the nook's one stool, he jacked it into the counter's power supply and accessed his mail.

He typed, *I'm up and open. Connect to this contact,* and sent the message across to the code Veronica had shown him.

He waited, trying not to fidget. He wished he'd thought to make a cup of coffee before he started, but now that he had started, he didn't want to leave the case. Anybody could come down the corridor and read the screen. He wanted all this cleared up, now.

Another line of text spelled itself out across the screen.

Up and open. Now, first question. What's anybody going to do with a CO_2 laser on Venus?

Josh felt his brows knit together. *What?*

What's the atmosphere out there made of? CO_2. What's going to happen if you fire a CO_2 laser into a CO_2 atmosphere? The beam is going to be absorbed almost immediately. What good is that going to be? The setup makes no sense!

Josh took a deep breath, steadying himself. A grand outburst was not going to accomplish anything. *We are obviously not seeing the whole mechanism. That's clear from the pattern of holes on the outside. There was something else here.*

Pause. He lifted his cap up, smoothed down his hair, and replaced it. New text appeared.

Dead convenient, isn't it? Anything that couldn't be cobbled together from local materials is conveniently missing from the scene, like a power source for the laser, like any kind of repeater or reflector that you couldn't make out of salt and stone. And what about the lights?

The lights? typed Josh, genuinely mystified.

The lights! There are three lights in the whole place and they're all in one room. Did somebody just climb down into the dark? Crawl through dark tunnels? Send messages in the dark?

Josh remembered her lying on her back in the antechamber, staring at the ceiling. Now genuine irritation flared. What did she want, a guidebook? They were supposed to be looking for possible answers for these questions. That was why they were all here. *This installation was built by aliens; we can't expect to understand their motives.*

No. That's the tautology whoever set this up wants us to start using. Anything that doesn't make sense can be put down to this all being done by aliens. OF COURSE it doesn't make sense to us.

Use Occam's Razor, Josh. What's the simpler explanation? That aliens came, undetected, to Venus and created an outpost, which they left half of in permanent darkness. Then they abandoned it, leaving just enough clues behind to let us know they were there. Or is the simpler truth that somebody set up a mysterious looking fake to gain some fame and fortune?

Or funding. Josh thought involuntarily. *Oh, Christ. Funding.*

His head felt light. The soft, background sounds of movement, random clanking, and soft conversation seemed unbearably loud. He tugged hard on the brim of his cap and looked over to the kitchen, wishing for coffee.

No. This was not happening. She was reading the data wrong.

More text spilled across the screen. *There is nothing in there we don't understand or that we couldn't make, given the proper facilities. Anything we might not understand is missing. It's a SETUP.*

Josh took a deep breath and forced his fingers to type in a reply. His hands had gone cold, he realized. *How come after weeks of camera work, measuring, tagging, and analysis, no one else has reached this conclusion?*

No one else wanted to, she replied.

Josh suppressed a snort. *And you did? Or maybe you just want to get back at Grandma Helen for thinking you're harmless?*

A long pause this time. A blank screen and a strained mental silence. *Is that what you think I'm doing?*

I think it's possible, returned Josh.

Fine. The connection shut down.

Josh sat there, staring at his screen, reading and rereading the words shining on its gray surface.

A fake? Impossible. Ridiculous. The amount of time, money, and material it would take to rig up a fake like this would be incredible. Nobody on Venera would have access to those kinds of resources.

Except maybe Grandma Helen.

Josh's spine stiffened. No. Now that really was crazy. She'd never do anything like this. No one would.

But, damn, hasn't it brought the money rolling in. Right when Venera needed it.

Josh shook his head. Crazy, crazy. The Venerans were scientists. If there was a cardinal sin among scientists, it was the falsification of data. If you got caught, it meant scandal, possible lawsuits, and the complete ruination of a career.

But if you didn't . . . Josh found he did not want to think about it. Anger darkened his mind. Vee'd done it. She'd stolen the day. Now, instead of wonder and excitement, he was filled up with suspicion and fear.

Josh slapped the case lid down. He stowed it away automatically, out of the habit of living and working in confined spaces. Then he shuffled sideways into the kitchen. No one else was there. He heard the sonic shower going. He heard voices from both sides and up front. He thought about coffee, but instead he opened the fridge and rummaged through the scarab's small stock of beer, pulled himself out a bottle, and twisted the top off.

"Everything all right, Josh?"

Josh turned. Adrian stood there, a suit glove in his hand.

"Yes and no." He sat at the table. Adrian put the glove on the table and reached into one of the overhead bins. "What's the matter with that?"

"Microfracture in one of the seals. Nothing big." He pulled down a tool kit and a plastic pack containing the silicon rings that helped seal the gloves to the joints in the suit cuffs.

Josh watched him work for a while; then he looked around carefully and said in a whisper. "Adrian, what do you think of our tourists?"

Adrian shrugged. "They're tourists," he murmured. Adrian had lots of practice at not being overheard. "They're looking for something profound or amazing to send back to Mother Earth. Saw it on Mars all the time. Idiots racing down Olympus Mons in go-carts and writing articles about what a deeply expanding experience it was." He frowned at the flawed seal for a moment. "Terry Wray's pretty cute though."

Josh chuckled. "If you like media bland."

"But it's such a cute kind of bland." Adrian inspected his work. "That'll do. I'm going to check the fit."

Adrian left him there and Josh sat alone listening to the comings and goings of the others. The air smelled of soap, sweat, minerals, and vaguely of sulfur. Josh glanced at the hatch to the couch compartment. What was she doing in there? Who was she telling her theory to? Her manager back on Earth? Julia or Troy, or one of the other team members?

Terry Wray and her camera?

Josh felt the blood rush from his face. If Vee told her ideas to anybody, *anybody,* there would be an outcry like nothing that had been heard yet. The Venerans, all of them, would stand accused of fraud. The U.N. would move in for real, work on the Discovery would be wrenched away, money would dry up, and Venera would fold, and work would stop because there would be no place to do the work from.

Stop it, Josh. What's a little more controversy?

Or are you starting to believe her? Are you starting to agree there's not one thing in the entire Discovery that could definitely not *have been made by a human with the time and resources?*

Josh swallowed hard. Feeling detached from himself, he got up and walked to the couch compartment and opened the hatch. The lights were down. Julia snored gently in her couch, one arm flung out into the aisle. Josh stepped around her.

Vee still sat up on her couch with her briefcase open on her knees. She glanced up briefly at him and then seemingly dismissed what she saw. Her hands never stopped moving across the command board.

"Don't," whispered Josh. "Don't go public with this."

"Why not?" she asked mildly.

"Because you'll ruin them. The Venerans."

"They deserve to be ruined." Bitterness swallowed all pretense of disinterest.

"All of them?" Josh leaned as close as he could. She had to hear him. He had to make her hear. "Everybody who lives in Venera deserves to be ruined? That's what'll happen."

Vee's hands stilled. "It's a fake, Josh. What do you want me to do? Perpetuate a fraud because the Venerans have been living beyond their means?"

Julia snorted and rolled over. Josh bit his tongue and waited until she subsided. "You don't give a shit about anybody but yourself, do you? You just want to show them all up. Noted artiste uncovers fraud where scientists fail. Click here to read."

Her face had gone perfectly smooth and expressionless. "Of course. What else would it be? It couldn't possibly be I believe what I'm saying or that I might be right."

Josh clamped his jaw shut around what he'd been about to say. Julia rolled again with a rustle of cloth and a sighing of breath. Josh glared at Vee as if he could make her see reason by sheer force of will. She just sat placidly, her face immobile, her eyes unimpressed.

Josh felt his teeth grind together. She'd do it. She'd ruin everything. Everything.

But what if she's right?

"What if I promised to go out now and mail Michael Lum? Tell him your suspicions, have him double-check to make sure all the funding's on the up and up. Would that satisfy you?"

Vee's gaze searched his face, considering. "It would be a start," she said at last.

Score one. "Would it at least keep you from telling Stykos and Wray about all this?" he pressed.

There was a long pause, and then Vee nodded.

"Okay, then." Josh unbent himself as far as the room allowed.

"Josh?" Vee's whisper stopped him.

"What?"

Her face was lost in shadow, so he could not make out her expression, but he heard the weight of her words. The anger, the flippancy had left, and all that remained was honest feeling—tired and a little worried. "I am not doing this to show anyone up. I am not doing this because I'm angry at Helen Failia. The Discovery has been falsified and whoever did it deserves whatever they get."

"We'll see."

He left her there and returned to the analysis nook, shaken and confused. She couldn't be right. But what if she was? Surely somebody had already investigated everything to make sure all was in order. But what if they hadn't?

His stomach tightened. *It's happening already. The idea's taking hold. Nothing to do but clear it out, one way or the other.*

Josh got his case down from its bin and brought it back to the analysis table, setting it down next to his half-finished beer. He jacked the case in, turned it on, took another swallow of beer, swore to himself, or maybe at himself, and started typing.

CHAPTER EIGHT

Michael rubbed the heels of both palms into his eyes. When he lowered them, he blinked hard and read Josh Kenyon's note again.

Dear Michael,

Sorry I can't do a v-mail, but this has got to be kept quiet. I spent the day working with Dr. Hatch, and she spent the day getting convinced that the Discovery is a fake.

I want to laugh at the idea, but I can't. She's making some good points, especially about the fact that there is nothing down here a human couldn't have made, given resources and time. There's also the fact that some facets of this laser we're studying don't make sense.

I know I'm not a Veneran, and I'd never tell you your job, but can you let me know you've checked everything out? The money's good, the logs are good, and so on? If I don't get something to tell Dr. Hatch, she might just go straight to the media drones.

Thanks,

Josh

* * *

Michael could picture Josh in the scarab, hunched over his case, swearing as he typed, not wanting to believe, but not being able to dismiss a reasonable premise without checking it out.

A hazard of the scientific mind.

And the security mind.

Had they checked for the possibility of fraud? Of course they had checked. That was the first thing they did after the governing board had come back up from the Discovery while the implications still made them all dizzy. Helen had run the money down. Ben had done the personnel logs. Michael had checked their checking, and everything looked fine. In the meantime, Helen had sent their best people down to the Discovery to start cataloging and looking for any sign of human intervention.

They'd turned up nothing, nothing, and more nothing.

Only then had Helen called the U.N.

So what was Veronica Hatch seeing? What possibility had they left open? Or was she just playing for the cameras? She might be the type. She certainly acted like the type.

It didn't make any difference, though. If this went into the stream, the accusations were going to fly, and everything Venera did regarding the Discovery would be called into question.

Michael stared out at the world beyond his desk. Administration was Venera's brain, even if the Throne Room was its heart. Unlike most of the workspace on the base, administration was not divided up into individual offices and laboratories. Each department had an open work section with desks scattered around it.

The arrangement made this one of the noisiest levels on Venera, second only to the education level. The idea was to keep everybody out in the open, so the left hand always knew what the right hand was doing. It met with limited success, but by now everyone was so used to it, no one really worked to change it.

As always, the place was a hive. A noisy hive of a thousand competing conversations, some with coworkers, some with residents or visitors who had complaints. His people wore no uniform, but they all had a white-and-gold badge pinned to their shirts to identify themselves.

He had forty people working for him right now, counting the U.N.'s contribution of Bowerman and Cleary. Since it was the day shift, about half of the security personnel were at their desks, dealing with complaints or paperwork or helping Venerans fill out forms for passports, marriage licenses, or taxes.

Only a handful of those people knew exactly how close they'd come to losing their home.

Or how close they still are, Michael chewed thoughtfully on his lower lip. *If the validity of the Discovery is called into question, the money flood is going to dry up, and we'll be right back where we started.*

Enough. The accusation had been made. The only question left was what to do about it.

First thing, revisit the evidence. Make sure the investigation was as complete as he thought it was four months ago. Second, check out Dr. Hatch. If she was doing this to call attention to herself, maybe she'd done similar things in the past. It might help to have that to hold up to her, or to anyone else who came calling.

Of course there was somebody on the base who knew all about Dr. Hatch. Michael pictured Philip Bowerman—a big man, serious, but with a sense of humor that ran just below the professional surface. From the beginning Bowerman and Cleary had been polite, circumspect, and very aware that they were unwelcome. Michael, in return, had made sure his people were polite, circumspect, and very aware that Bowerman and Cleary were just doing their job.

Still, the idea of going to the yewners with this made his stomach curdle.

And not because you're worried you might have let something slide past that they'll catch. Oh, no.

Michael straightened up. "Desk. Contact Philip Bowerman." Bowerman was wired for sound, as were most U.N. security people. He and Cleary had given Michael their contact codes within minutes of his meeting them.

"Bowerman," the man's voice came back. "How can I help you, Dr. Lum?"

"I've got one or two questions about the U.N. team to ask you."

"Okay," said Bowerman without hesitation. "I'm in the Mall, but I'll be right up."

"No, that's okay. I'll come down."

Eleven years as head of security had given Michael a refined appreciation of how Venera's rumor mill worked. There would actually be less talk if Michael "ran into" Bowerman at the Mall than if he sat closeted with the man at his desk behind sound dampeners. Lack of talk was something much to be desired right now, especially with Stykos and his camera band roaming the halls.

"Desk," said Michael as he stood. "Display Absence Message 1. Record and store all incoming messages, or if the situation is an emergency, route to my personal phone."

"Will comply," said the desk. Its screen displayed the words AT LUNCH, LEAVE A MESSAGE.

Michael tucked his phone spot into his ear and threaded his way between the desks, heading for the stairs.

Michael walked down past the farms, past the gallery level with its harvester and processing plants, its winery, brewery, bakery, and butchery, past the research level, and past two of the residential levels with their concentric rings of brightly painted doors, and past the educational level where the irrepressible sound of children's voices rang off the walls. Below the educational level waited the Mall.

From the beginning, Venera had been designed to support whole families. Helen had wanted people to be able to make a long-term commitment to their work. The open Mall with its shops, trough gardens, food stalls, and cafe-like seating clusters was one of the features that made the base livable for years at a time.

The Mall was about half full. An undercurrent of voices thrummed through the air, along with scents of cooking food, coffee, and fresh greenery. Meteorologists clustered around a table screen, probably getting readings of a storm from the sampling equipment Venera carried in its underbelly. Off-shift techs and engineers played cards, typed letters, ate sandwiches, or sipped coffee. Graduate students took advice and instructions from senior researchers, and senior researchers tossed ideas back and forth between each other. A pod of science feeders held a whispered argument among themselves. If the gestures were anything to go by, it was getting pretty heated. Families, knots of friends, and loners drifted in and out of the shops or stood in line at the food booths. Around the edges of the hall, a couple of maintenancers spritzed the miniature trees and dusted off the grow-lights. A cluster of children played with puzzle bricks at their parents' feet. If anyone's gaze landed on him, they waved or nodded and he returned their greetings reflexively. Michael no longer knew the names of everyone on Venera, but he knew most of the faces, and he couldn't bring himself to think of anyone aboard the base as a stranger.

This was his world. It was not the only one he had ever known, but it was the only one that had ever truly known him.

Spotting Bowerman took only a quick scan of the room. The man stood out in his subdued blue-and-white tunic. Venerans went in for bright colors.

Bowerman had picked a table near the far edge of the Mall under a pair of potted orange trees. He spotted Michael before Michael was halfway across the floor and lifted a hand.

"Please, sit down." Bowerman gestured toward the empty chair as Michael reached him. "Mind if I go ahead?" he nodded at his lunch—soup, fresh bread, a cup of rich *chai,* spiced Indian tea that Margot at Salon Blu imported.

"Please. I'm actually going to meet my wife for lunch right after this."

"You two have kids?" asked Bowerman, breaking apart his small loaf of sourdough bread and spreading it thickly with butter.

"Two boys," said Michael, going with the conversation and not bothering to mention that Bowerman surely knew this from reading Michael's files. "You?"

Bowerman shook his head. "Not yet." He bit into the bread, chewed, and swallowed. "This is good. I didn't expect such good food, or so much space." He gestured with the bread. "I've only been to Small Step on Luna, and on Mars once. I got used to the idea that colonies are cramped."

Michael noticed Bowerman did not say where he'd been on Mars. "Our one real luxury," he said, repeating the stock phrase.

"So." Bowerman put the bread down and picked up his soup spoon. "How can I help you?"

Good question. Michael hesitated. He'd made up his mind to do this while he was behind his desk, but now that he faced Bowerman, he had trouble putting the words together. He was about to tell the U.N. there might be a problem aboard Venera. Venera was a colony, and the U.N. looked for excuses to make life difficult for colonies. That was a fact. What if Michael was about to give them such an excuse?

Bowerman wasn't looking at him. He concentrated on his soup, making little appreciative slurping noises as he ate. *I could get up and leave. I could invent something small and leave, go tell Helen what's going on, and let her handle it. I could do that.*

"One of the investigative team has raised a question about the validity of the Discovery."

Bowerman paused and set his spoon down. "Oh?" The syllable could have meant anything from "Oh, really?" to "Only one?"

Going to make me say it, aren't you? Okay, I'd do the same if I were you. "We investigated this exact question extensively when the Discovery first came to our attention. I assume you saw the reports?"

Bowerman's gaze turned sharp. Michael had his full attention now. "They looked thorough. Do you think you missed something?"

Michael sighed. He appreciated the lack of judgment in Bowerman's voice. Just one pro talking to another. Anybody could miss something. It happened. "I don't know," he admitted. "But if a fraud accusation is going to be made, that isn't good enough. I have to know."

Bowerman nodded soberly. "How can we help?"

Michael studied his fingertips. The scent of beef and tomatoes reached him from Bowerman's soup and his stomach rumbled. "If this is a fraud, it cost money," he said slowly. "And Venera was running on a wing, a prayer, and short credit. If somebody did this, they got money from somewhere."

"Or shuffled it from somewhere," said Bowerman quietly.

Michael just nodded.

"Who could do that?"

"Most easily?" Michael didn't look up. He didn't want to see Bowerman's eyes, weighing, calculating, running ahead with different scenarios to see how each of them might fit. "I could. Ben Godwin or Helen Failia. After us, the department heads."

"But Dr. Failia is in charge of base finance, isn't she?"

Michael nodded again. Helen had kept that position for herself. She raised the money, she counted the money, she divvied the money up. It was no small task, but she would not delegate it. Occasionally, Michael suspected Helen did not want to admit she was not entirely in control of this city of ten thousand.

Bowerman was silent for a long time. "All right. I'll call down to Earth and start a trace on the incoming funds for, say, the year before the Discovery's announcement. Will that do?"

Now Michael looked up. Bowerman's face was understanding but not pitying, which he also appreciated. "How quiet can you keep this?"

"I'll do my best," he shrugged. "But I have to tell my boss."

"Who will have to tell the Venus work group?"

Bowerman nodded one more time. "But trust me, they will not want to let this out until they're sure. There've been a lot of speeches made about your Discovery, and nobody's going to want to look like they bought vaporware. We'll sell it as double-checking your facts. Just doing our job." He smiled thinly. "Everybody knows we don't trust your kind."

Michael gave a short laugh. "So they do."

"I'd recommend two other things." Bowerman tapped the table gently with his spoon. "First you let me ask my boss, Sadiq Hourani, to order an audit of Venera's books. If we go over it all, when we find nothing, no one will be able to accuse you of hiding anything. Also, if Angela and I do it, well . . ." He smiled again. "We can be obnoxious. We don't live here and nobody likes us anyway."

"Good idea," admitted Michael. "What's the other thing?"

"Let me get Angela checking around the team down there.

See if anything suspicious is going on, let her talk to Hatch, and so on. See what the position is on the ground."

"Also good," Michael paused. "I don't suppose you can let me have what you've got on Dr. Hatch, can you?"

Bowerman's stirred his soup, considering. "I might be able to leave a file unsecured here and there."

"Thanks." Michael's phone spot rang the two-tone reminder chime. Michael tapped it in acknowledgment, gratefully. "I've got to go. I'm meeting my wife."

"Go." Bowerman waved the spoon. "I'll stop by tomorrow. Let you know what the preliminary view is."

"Thanks," said Michael again. "I appreciate it."

Bowerman smiled his acknowledgment and returned his attention to his cooling soup.

Michael didn't hang around. He headed for the nearest stairwell and climbed back up toward the educational level. Jolynn was headmaster for grades one through six and they were going to have lunch in her office. She was having it brought in.

He tried not to think. He tried to blank the conversation he'd just had out of his mind and concentrate on the outside world—the voices, the faces, the sights that he knew as well as any man from Mother Earth knew the rooms of his house or the streets of his city. He'd grown up here with tilt drills, suit drills, and evacuation drills. He'd always known that inside was safe, and outside was poison.

But he'd never believed that the outside could touch him, not really.

He'd been on Earth when his father died. For the first time, he was walking under a sky that rained water, not acid. He was breathing air that didn't come from a processing plant and seeing the stars at night. He was infatuated with Mother Earth.

His mother's v-mail came. Dad had had one of those accidents they warned you about. Venus had used one of her thousand tricks to kill him or take down his scarab. Same thing. There was nothing to bury, nothing to burn. Just a lifetime of memories ringing around his head and Mom asking him to come home.

He went. But he swore not to stay. He went so he could attend the memorial service and help sort out the will and all the other red tape death generates. All his remaining energies he bent toward trying to convince Mom to come back to Earth. She'd been born there, after all, and she was getting old, despite the med trips. Since long-life was not something she wanted for herself, what was keeping her there, in a world that would kill her?

Come down, come back, come home. This home. Our real home, where Michael was going back to and fully intended to stay.

"You do what you have to, Michael," she said. "And grant me the right to do the same."

"This is no place for a human being to live, Mom. Trapped in a bubble like this."

She'd sighed, with that annoying infinite patience she was capable of. "Some trap. The door's open Michael. Go or stay, it's all up to you." She'd taken his hands then. "I love you, Son. If you want to live on Earth, then that's what you should do." She'd meant it too, every word.

So Michael had gone. He'd finished his degree, he'd found work, and within a year, he'd come back to Venus, found work again, met Jolynn, and gotten married.

He'd never questioned what he'd done, but he'd never really understood it either. He'd never been able to point to any one thing and say, "That was it; that was why I left Earth." He'd been lonely, it was true, and the vast global village of Earth with its snarl of republics could be confusing to some-